PLUM TREE LANE

Plum Tree Lane

Lodwick Hartley

The Sandlapper Store, Inc.

History is not what you thought it was. It is what you can remember. All other history defeats itself.

W. C. Sellar and R. J. Yeatman

The life of a man is of no greater importance to the universe than that of an oyster.

David Hume

FOREWORD

I have called this book chapters in a fictional memoir rather than a series of autobiographical chapters because, though the characters presented are derived from real people (as all good fictional characters are), they are not intended to be taken for anything other than characters in a fictional account. The teller of the tale is, moreover, a persona rather than the author; and the events that he recounts are not designed to be true in every detail.

Such a method, I would hope, would not undercut my real purpose, which is to document a brief period of enormous world change (1906-1918) by reflecting this change ironically and humorously against the life of a small Southern town as seen through the eyes of a narrator whose entrance into the world and whose childhood coincide with the limits of the selected era. In order to achieve such an objective I have abandoned strict chronological sequence in favor of a plan that generally observes time sequence but in which chapters are treated as discrete familiar essays with narrative intent or, in two instances, short stories. (Chapter IV, "The Day of the Octopus," appeared in the *University of Kansas City Review,* and Chapter VI, "Miss Malvina: An Interlude," was published in the *Georgia Review*, both under slightly different forms.)

In a much earlier day, Horace Walpole observed, "The world is a comedy to those who think, a tragedy to those who feel." Whether or not this statement is universally true I do not venture to say. But I do argue that it is possible to go back with feeling to a segment of the past and still to relish its comedy. Such is the essential purpose of this "memoir."

L.H.

CONTENTS

I

BORN POST-VICTORIAN

EUGENE LONESCO has a character in *The Bald Soprano* who complains that newspapers always tell how old people are when they die but never how old they are when they are born. Obviously, everybody is extremely old when he is born, though methods of computing the age may vary widely and may suggest too many complications for comfort. A person might, of course, say that he is as old as the world, or date himself from the time the first creature climbed out of the ocean on his upward journey toward intelligent life—or maybe with the appearance of the initial bit of deoxyribonucleic acid. But these things boggle the mind and are in the bailiwick of the scientists and philosophers who like to play with such questions. They are definitely not for me.

Thus I have no idea how old I was when I was born on Tuesday, June 12, 1906, a little after midnight. I can merely assume that I inherited not only a certain mixture of genes but also a social, moral, cultural, and economic environment over which I had no control and which had been around for a considerable time before I opened my eyes to a light that took me some time to comprehend—if, indeed, I ever did.

As important as the day was to me (as well as to some of the more than one hundred thousand people who were born on the same day in various parts of the world), it was not otherwise of great significance. This is not to say that to some people fairly well launched in life it did not have its glamor. One might take for example the young Nicholas Longworths, who had been honeymooning in Europe, and especially Mrs. Longworth, whom as the daughter of President Theodore Roosevelt the London newspapers were beginning to call "Princess Alice." On June 12, the American Ambassador Whitelaw Reid and his wife gave a glittering party at the Dorchester House to allow the distinguished visitors to meet Edward VII—or the other way around. The guest list appropriately included four dukes (three with their duchesses), a half dozen or more peers of the realm, and a scattering of distinguished baronets and knights, not to mention members of the American aristocracy and family connections like the Ogden Millses.

On the day before the twelfth, and certainly spilling over into it, had also come one of the biggest weddings of the New York social season when Cynthia Roche married Arthur Scott Burden at Grace Church and the Roches gave a splendid reception afterward at Sherry's—adequately covered in all the New York newspapers. On the eleventh, too, the *Times* reported less happy news about another local Social Registerite: Frank J. Gould was arrested for speeding on the way from New York to Lyndhurst and was released after posting a one-hundred dollar bond. The American liner *Westernland* had run aground off the Delaware Capes with 880 passengers on board, but it had been refloated. More tragic was the story of the *Atlantic City Express* which, traveling at fifty miles an hour, had jumped the track, killing one and injuring scores of passengers.

On the eleventh the Giants had won over

Cincinnati 1 to 0, but on the twelfth they lost ignominiously to the same team 6 to 0—a bad day for all true fans. Police were reporting that clues were scarce for solving the murder of Mrs. Alice Kennan in the Bronx; and dispatches from Russia indicated that the Czar's position was being undermined by a revolt of troops at Poltava and near mutiny at Kursk.

Mme. Sarah Bernhardt, with her wooden leg, was giving another of her "Farewells" at the Lyric Theater in New York; and the *Times* critic was to write a ho-hum account of the scenes she presented from *Hamlet* (playing the melancholy prince, of course) and *L'Aiglon* (in the role of the tragic young son of Napoleon), as well as scenes from *Meilac* and *Frou-Frou.*

While his daughter was touring Europe expensively, the President himself was explaining to the press that his travel allowance of $25,000 per annum would be used strictly for official purposes, not one dime for personal ones. The *Times* in a lengthy editorial found the idea on the whole reasonable.

Plus ça change, plus c'est même chose, the French have been reported as saying. But maybe not quite.

June 12 had been preceded by one of the greatest cataclysms between the Lisbon earthquake and the bombing of Hiroshima—namely, the earthquake and fire in San Francisco on April 18 and 19; and it was to be followed on June 25 by an almost comparable shock to eastern American society when Harry K. Thaw shot Stanford White on the Winter Garden Roof in New York, allegedly over the actress Evelyn Nesbit.

But all these things that happened before, on, and after June 12 were not where I was or likely to be for some time to come. What was going on more appositely in the small town in which I was born I could, I suppose, find out if I did the proper amount of research. There was a local newspaper called the *Advocate,* of which there may still be brown and tattered files somewhere. But they are not preserved on microfilm as the files of *The New York Times* are; and searching out the social and political happenings of the town at the time might entail more pain than profit.

The *Advocate* did bring out an illustrated issue, for some unspecified occasion in 1902, which is available and which gives certain pertinent general details that probably had not changed materially in the four years between its appearance and my birth. (Times had a way of not changing as quickly at the beginning of the century as they have been doing since.) An excerpt or two from the historical sketch written by a local worthy should be inserted at this point:

> In the year Anno Domini 1869 [the village Latinist is a bit redundant], the town of Bayesville was laid out. It was named in honor of Capt. A.D. Bayes, who was one of the moving spirits in those days for the advancement of the community.
>
> In the fall of 1868, or early in 1869, the old Charlotte, Columbia, and Augusta Railroad was completed from Columbia to Augusta and at that time each X-road wanted a depot. Through the efforts of Mr. Derwent Barclay (my great uncle) . . . and Capt. A. D. Bayes . . . the management of the railroad was induced to establish a depot.
>
> Bayesville is a town now of about 1500 inhabitants, situated on the famous Ridge Belt, thirty-three miles from Columbia and fifty-three from Augusta. The climate is all that could be wished. The people, as a general thing, all enjoy good health. [Comforting but not entirely true.]

The fact that the town was named for an ex-officer in the Confederate Army just four or five years away from the War was both appropriate and typical. My great uncle who was a large landowner and who lived in the biggest and most historic house in town (built in 1785, according to the historical marker) seems to have made no claim on the honor.

The account in the *Advocate* predictably goes on to speak of the productive soil of the region and the advantage there for either "agricultural or mechanical pursuits." The growth of the place had been phenomenal (for the time), from three stores, four houses, and a hotel in 1872 to the relative metropolis it was in 1902—with an annual average growth of about fifty people! The hotel, by the way, kept by Capt. Bayes and Mr. John Perry, was a railroad eating house where trains stopped for twenty minutes at the proper times for breakfast, dinner, and supper—indicating remarkably handsome commuting service between village and cities for so early a date.

In 1902 my father was forty-four years old. He had started life as a farmer on land that my grandfather had given him. Then after he had produced one child—a son who for a long time seemed destined to be the sole heir—he moved to town and set up a merchandising business with a maiden sister as a partner. The *Advocate* of 1902 carried a fairly large advertisement for Paul T. Barclay & Company, General Merchandising, advising initially that—

> Our Motto: is to try to give our trade the most for the money and make every trade agreeable. We carry a full stock of Shoes, Hats, Clothing, Notions, Dry Goods, and Fine Crockery, that you can always find bargains in.

The larger section of the advertisement announced in bold letters that the firm was agent for Walter A. Wood harvesting machines, "the best and longest lasting machines on the market." An impressive cut of one of the machines filled the rest of the space.

My father, then, was forty-eight when my mother's eccentric physician-brother brought me into the world head first and delivered the standard blow to my bottom—a stout blow, if I may judge from my experience with an uncle that I was in my later years to regard as a medical masochist. At the time my parent had succeeded fairly well in business and he was getting ready to send his seventeen-year-old son to Clemson College to study electrical engineering. Since he himself had had very little education, he was determined that his son should not have the same handicap. My mother was forty-one, and the first presage of my being on the way had produced, surprise, unbelief, and shock, I think in that order. One of my aunts later confided to me that my mother's first notion was that she was developing some sort of tumor. Certainly, after so many years she could not readily admit the idea that she was pregnant.

I am not sure that she ever fully got over the surprise or that she ever completely believed in my existence, unless it was in her last years when her stout independence was all but eroded and when she was willing to accept gratefully the reality I afforded in producing moral and other kinds of support not easily available from her older son, by then married and seemingly far away. The person who was pleased most by my arrival was my maiden aunt, who was ready at the outset to deluge me with the kind of devotion that was a natural compensation for barrenness.

At this time, I had better sketch in my family—including Aunt Allie, who though not actually living under our roof was very much in the family picture. As a late-comer I was, of course, a little creature who seemed destined to be forever surrounded by an adult world, with parents who could have been my grandparents and a brother who could biologically have been my father—even though I was for a long time only barely conscious of these circumstances.

My mother was a small woman, just a little over five feet in height and weighing not much over a hundred pounds. She had a mildly swarthy complexion and thin, curly dark hair—which, incidentally, hardly changed color at all even after she was over eighty. In fact, I have the impression that she was always the same age, and I could not conceive of her as ever having been young. The only evidence I have of her youth is a little autograph album, bound in dark red leather and embossed in a design of gold curlicues. In it were not only the autographs of her friends, both male and female, but also "sentiments" written by them most often in a florid, shaded hand and decorated with labels depicting vases, cornucopias, and baskets of flowers and bearing rhymed mottos like "As the scent of roses pure, so will my love for you endure." As a sort of prologue to the book, my mother at the age of seventeen on July 8, 1883, had written, or rather copied, the following:

> To My Friends
> My album is a garden spot,
> Where all my friends may sow,
> Where thorns and thistles flourish not
> But flowers alone may grow.
> With sunshine (smiles?) for sunshine, tears for showers,
> I'll water, watch, and tend these flowers.

Scores of such "flowers" of rhetoric follow—"sentiments" such as friends, male and female, and relatives wrote over and over again with absolutely no originality in hundreds of albums. My father's entry was a birthday verse written in a plain hand and without an ornamental label:

> I wish thee every blessing
> That can attend thee here
> And may each future birthday
> Prove my wish to be sincere.

How many of the other males who wrote in the album were suitors of my mother, I have no way of telling, flowery sentiments in such instances meaning very little. I do know that my father had to wait for five more birthdays before he snared his prey.

Like every child, I must have thought of my mother as being pretty. But the only reliable picture I have of her, taken about a decade before my birth, shows her to be prim and neat rather than beautiful in any sense. Among her aversions (and she had a variety of them) was one to the camera. I don't know how my father or anybody else ever persuaded her to go to a studio for a "family" portrait, such as the one in my possession, made with an idyllic garden backdrop. My father with a receding hairline and a bushy mustache wore a dark suit with a white shirt, turndown collar, and small flowered bow-tie. Standing between his parents, my brother looked like Little Lord Fauntleroy in a short-pants suit with a bow-tie almost as large as he was. My mother had chosen a dark blue woolen dress, tight at the waist, with large puffed sleeves, and a shawl-like collar—the whole neatly trimmed with ric-rac braid. All three people had the look of having just barely turned off the expressions of annoyance and discomfort that they really felt. Never afterward was anybody able to persuade my mother to go before a camera. The best we could ever do was to get an occasional snapshot when she was not looking.

Pretty, then, she was not. Pleasant and bright she could often be. And determined she always was. She had simple and, therefore, narrow views of life. Most of all she hated sham and pretention. Any kind of compliment given to her face had to be couched in subtleties or delivered by indirection; otherwise it was likely to be regarded as fulsome and hypocritical. If she had any kind of vanity, she succeeded in masking it artfully.

She believed in the Puritan ethic of work and never doubted that a woman's place is in the home. I am afraid, nevertheless, that, like most women of her time and since, she regarded herself as something of a martyr. I would judge so from her quoting a little too often, "A man's work is from sun to sun; a woman's work is never done." And I regret to report that she relished other such bits of copy-book morality as "An idle mind is the devil's workshop" and that she embroidered on two pillowslips to be used on the guest-room bed: "I slept and dreamed that life was beauty" (on one), "I woke and found that life was duty" (on the other). She was also fond of aiming at me such a line as "Procrastination is the thief of time." Whether she had read Young's Night Thoughts from which it was pilfered, I do not know; but she would have appreciated both the mood and the theology of that unconscionably long poem.

Busy she always was, but never with the kind of busyness that Robert Louis Stevenson regarded as a sign of deficient vitality. Of energy she had God's plenty. When she was not in the kitchen concocting wonderful delicacies or cooking the world's most palatable staple foods, she was (armed with dust cloth, mop, and Old Dutch Cleanser) deep in housework, or on her knees under a frilled bonnet or a straw hat in the flower garden pulling up crab grass and weeds and resetting plants. Like every woman in town, she had a siesta in the afternoon between two and four. But when she reappeared fresh and neat in the late afternoon in the front-hall sitting-room or in a rocking chair on the front piazza, her hands were never idle. There was always a crochet needle or an embroidery hoop or a pan of English peas to be shelled for the next day's midday meal. No round little worm would ever be pricked from a lazy finger of hers. Not only did she scorn card-playing women who left kitchens and children to servants, but she also did not approve of those who went to too many meetings of their church circles or missionary societies. Both types of indulgence smacked of indolence and vanity.

As one would quickly guess, if she was a rigid disciplinarian in regard to herself, she was also in regard to me. If I went out in the morning spic and span, as I had to be at my morning inspection, I was supposed to return almost as spic and span. If I did not, I made reparations in some way—often taking a switching, a favorite device of punishment. (At my house the application of a hairbrush to a bottom was considered vulgar.) Because of this well-nigh impossible regimen, I got a great deal of assistance and sympathy from mothers of my playmates who would do remarkable things to enable me to go home as if a minimum of mussing had taken place. I have one particularly fond memory of a morning when I joined several of my friends in stealing rides on the tailgates of wagons carrying cotton from farm to market on a little dirt road near my house. Jumping and missing my mark on this occasion, I landed supine, smack in the middle of a considerable mud puddle. Needless to say, I was splattěred from head to foot. What should I do? No problem, one of my playmates assured me! Taking me by the hand, he marched me a block or two up the street to his own house, where his mother had her cook wash my clothes, dry them miraculously quickly behind the kitchen range, and iron them, while in the meantime my mother was called to tell her that I was having lunch with my friend. So in the afternoon I went home with complete confidence. My mother never knew what had happened; and from that time on I shared a secret and a joke with a large segment of the neighborhood.

There were numerous other things that other children did that I could not do. I couldn't jump up and down on beds and sofas. I couldn't bring friends into the house without asking permission and I couldn't rummage in closets or attic for old clothes to be used for "dressing up" or impromptu theatricals. I was not supposed to raid the pantry or ice box, and so on. Not that I never did such things. I simply had to be extra-careful in not getting caught. Yet with all my restrictions, I don't remember being over-rebellious or resentful; and my psyche was not scarred. In fact, my impressions are of a happy rather than a repressed and unhappy childhood.

Maybe the reason is that I had a good deal of support and indulgence from other members of my family.

Aunt Allie, of course, could usually be counted on to take my side and to mollify punishments decreed for me whenever she was aware of them and could do so. In many respects she was as neat and precise as my mother. If anything, in looks she was somewhat plainer. I have a snapshot of her with my mother and me (still in long dresses) sitting on our front doorsteps. There, it is true, she looked quite smart in a *Godey's-Lady's-Book* way, with a light colored dress full in skirt and blouse and very tight in the waist and with a hat poised like a boat full of flowers ready to set sail from her generous hair-do. Of my father's other sisters, or brothers for that matter, I knew relatively few; for most of the siblings of the large family had died before I was born. The really pretty sister was Aunt Clarina, who lived out of town during much of my early childhood but who as a widow had a house next door to us later on. Tall and slender, with dark hair and bright black eyes, she appeared not only beautiful but aristocratic. Perhaps because my father admired her greatly, both my mother and Aunt Allie sometimes ill concealed their jealousy.

I have no idea whether Aunt Allie ever had serious beaux, though she was sometimes teased about having a rustic lover. She gave the impression of being born an old maid. But though she might have been immaculate in appearance and in morals and though she was deeply religious (she rarely missed church and she taught a Sunday School class for children for many years), she was never straight-laced or overtly pious. It is characteristic that the book she liked best was Augusta Evans's *St. Elmo*, a novel that had been read by thousands of Southen women, married and unmarried, since it came out in 1867. It is an excessively sentimental story about an orphan named Edna Earl, who was taken into the home of Mrs. Murray, widow of a Georgia planter and mother of an arrogant, dissipated son who, as one would expect, fell in love with his mother's ward. I am sure that Aunt Allie empathized and identified with the heroine perfectly. What could have been more appealing to a spinster than the idea of the reformation of a handsome, wicked, and atheistic male—Pamela's Mr. B— and Clarissa's Lovelace rolled into one? And how little she would have understood D.H. Lawrence's diabolic idea on the other side that the "greatest triumph an American woman can have is the triumph of seducing a man, especially if he is pure."

She had dedicated her life to my father and then, as an extension of the same affection, to me. Leaving out the literary connection (of which there was surely less than none), the relationship, I later decided, was not entirely unlike that of William and Dorothy Wordsworth. My mother would have played the part of Mary Hutchinson reasonably well and would have in all probability like Mary have accepted my aunt as a fellow-traveler on the honeymoon. As a constant companion and helper in the store Aunt Allie was indispensable to my father. Behind the counter in her white and soberly frilled cotton apron, or sometimes in an ecru one, she was so ingratiatingly efficient and competent that she developed a large clientele of local women who depended on her to supply them with the latest fashions in piece goods, ribbons, and notions.

When she died, I was just entering high school. I can remember my father's infinitely forlorn face as I sat with him in a semi-darkened room after the funeral and his single remark, just a fraction away from a sob: "She was the best woman I ever knew."

The easiest way to describe my father is to say directly that he was a gentle, kind, and uncomplicated man who gave himself to hard work and his little family. Had he not moved to town and gone into something so unromantic as shop-keeping, he might have been a character out of Rousseau or Wordsworth. "Intense and frugal, apt for all affairs," he might have been like the shepherd of Grasmere vale named Michael—except for the fact that he was no physical giant. Rather was he a tall, thin man who in spite of his capacity for physical labor in the vegetable garden, around the house, or in the store, gave the impression of frailty.

He had little formal education and he was almost entirely unbookish. The only book he read regularly—and that never ostentatiously—was the Bible. Another book was *Pilgrim's Progress,* published in a large quarto edition. From this he would at times read to me, allowing me to sit on his lap and turn the pages, and to pause as long as I chose to look with fascination and sometimes in terror at the Dore engravings (Apollyon, for example, with his horrible face, heavily veined bat wings, and smoke coming out of his belly).

According to a story, there is in a Charleston, South Carolina, churchyard an eighteenth-century lady's tombstone bearing the inscription: "She was pious without enthusiasm." If the eighteenth-century rather than the later meaning of enthusiasm were applied, this could be my father's epitaph. As my mother would have said, he had religion but not church. Yet he believed that attendance on the Sunday morning preaching service was mandatory, not only for himself but, less fortunately, for me. (My mother was so successful in convincing him that her role was Martha's rather than Mary's that she was excused.) The rule was to pick me up after Sunday School and plant me in my father's pew where I usually squirmed in boredom over what seemed to be interminable sermons. I was often switched for my squirming when I got home. This punishment I regarded as indicating one of the few flaws in my father's character, but I never cherished resentment for a long time. In other respects I could count on his indulgence; and as a result I felt that I loved him much more extravagantly than I did my mother.

If his slight obeisance to orthodoxy brought some unpleasantness to me, an evidence of a minor slip into heterodoxy was entirely endearing. In spite of the fact that he was a Baptist and a member of a congregation that was not loath to "turn out" members for various and often minor infractions of doctrine or rules (a process not entirely unlike Catholic excommunication), he liked his toddy and had it on proper occasions. Yet he was not a steady drinker. It was chiefly in cold weather that whiskey (bourbon, to be sure) appeared in our house. On an extremely cold evening, out might come a little glass jug, a sugar bowl, and a steaming tea kettle. Although my mother brought in the ingredients and the glasses, as a practicing but not a doctrinaire teetotaler she did not participate. But I was allowed to pull up my little chair and to be served a toddy, largely water and sugar with a drop or two of whiskey. I am told that the experience very nearly made an addict of me; for one day when I was sick and was being bathed with rubbing alcohol to reduce my fever, I got a good whiff of the delightful odor and became indignant that the remedy was not being administered to my interior rather than to my exterior. Thereupon I demanded a toddy. I got it. Though it was not winter and thus there was no potable alcohol in the house, a female cousin who lived next door and who had dropped in for a visit hurried home and produced enough liquor from her cellarette to meet my immediate needs.

Such precocious depravity might have been expected to lead to an early appearance on skid row. But it did not. Actually the fact that liquor and wines (the latter almost exclusively of the home-made variety) were never regarded extraordinary or wicked at our house gave them no special charm for me—the usual appeal of the forbidden. And somehow the taste for whiskey that I developed as a very small child soon vanished—not to reemerge for many years. It might have been due (as I now think of it) to a device slyly pulled on me by my mother. As I knew to my frequent sorrow, castor oil was regarded as a sovereign remedy for almost everything. With its heavy, horrible, gagging qualities it had the worst taste in the world, and I could be counted on to resist the administering of it with all the noise and violence of a little savage. Other mothers disguised it, or tried to disguise it for their children by mixing it with orange juice. My mother did so by using blackberry wine. Is there any wonder that for years I regarded all wines, and by extension all other alcoholic beverages, with nausea?

With my father, mother, and aunt taken care of for the time being, only my brother is left. I wish that I could do a better job of describing him, but I am limited by the fact that all during my childhood I saw him relatively little and then chiefly when he was at home on vacation from college or from his work at distant places like Pittsburgh or New York. I always had a hard time regarding him as anything but a visitor, a mature one whom I constantly addressed as "Sir" as if he were my father or no relation to me at all. Yet from my toddler stage I idolized him, feeling that he was unusually handsome, fascinating, and gifted. His extant college pictures, indeed, do show him to be good looking. He was of medium height and he had my mother's dark hair and tinge of brownness in his skin. He rode me on his shoulder and back, he played games with me (some of his own invention), he bought toys for me downtown or, even better, made them for me out of scraps of wood and wire. I was disappointed if I could not tag along with him wherever he went. I thought him charming and clever, but I never felt that I really knew him. Most of the time he was away out there in the distance. He was somebody who sent letters to be read at our dinner table, or little and big surprise presents for me, or who might galvanize the household into roasting and baking or other forms of activity by announcing a coming visit. Trains took on added romance by the possibility of his arrival on them; and the aroma of cigars and pipes, wherever I encountered it, reminded me of the delicate odor of tobacco that remained in our house for weeks after he had left us. Yet he never seemed to have a palpable reality.

Such was the immediate family in which I found myself: a small, modest, respectable, and entirely undistinguished one. A cousin who enjoyed being family historian and genealogist was much later to remind me that my father's family had had interesting connections with Charleston before one member, my direct ancestor, struck out for the wilderness of mid-South Carolina. One member of the early family, in fact, had a fine house on the Battery (it is still there) and a plantation called Hyde Park at Jacksonborough. A son of this family was sent to Oxford for his education, and another member of the family, an organist at St. Michael's Church and a composer of some ability, was a firm Loyalist who went back to England during the Revolution. The records show, however, that my own grandfather of whatever degree of "greatness" and whatever age at the time, was not more than a private during the affray; so no chance of making the Society of the Cincinnati was offered here! It was also rumored that on my mother's side a grandfather had put on a coonskin cap, shouldered a flint-lock rifle, and joined General Francis Marion to fight the Red Coats in the

South Carolina Swamps. But this kind of stuff was not part of the conversation at our house. My mother did not approve of such nonsense. Her view had been ably expressed by Nathaniel Hawthorne in *The House of Seven Gables:*

> Once in every half-century, at longest, a family should be merged into the great, obscure mass of humanity, and forget all about its ancestors.

So, as far as my mother had anything to do with it, ours did forget.

II

EDEN IS THAT OLD-FASHIONED HOUSE

IT is not easy for anyone to determine when he first became conscious of the magic, funny, and sometimes terrible world in which he finds himself. Somehow I have the persistent first memory of swinging on the gate of a white picket fence that surrounded our front yard. I am holding on to a little tin bucket and shovel such as children use in beach sand. Down the cool shady street stretch the white-washed trunks of willow oaks that line both sides, suggesting soldiers in dress whites with enormous green shakos, standing for inspection. It is summer, and out of the shade the sun is hot.

This is not much of a memory. It should include, though for some unknown reason it does not, an important person who was surely in the background, careful that I should not fall. This was Leila, my black nurse, whom I grew to regard as one of the most beautiful and important people in what I knew of the world—one person who would protect me, steal goodies for me, and comfort me when life, or my mother's interpretation of it, seemed too hard to bear.

The house, too, was in the background, with a personality all its own. Emily Dickinson wrote with her usual perceptiveness—

> Eden is that old-fashioned house
> We dwell in every day
> Without suspecting our abode
> Until we drive away.

Our "abode" was modest enough from any point of view. It was a one-story white clapboard cottage with green blinds, flanked by two magnolia trees and surrounded by a yard that always seemed to have flowers in it. Inside, there were only five or six rooms, but they were very large rooms; and through the middle of the house ran a wide hall that, divided in the middle, made two informal living areas to supplement the parlor at the front of the house. A front piazza with a swing and several rocking chairs provided an outdoor living space. Shielded as it was by a vine-covered trellis and innumerable ferns on shelves and stands, from it one could have a reasonably good view of the street without being seen in return.

As small as the area was, my first impression of it was that it was a maze or jungle, crowded with furniture and indefinable objects around which I had to find my way. In the summertime when the hall was open at both ends, it was easier to know where I was; and it was pleasant to roam around or to lie about on floors covered with cool straw matting. In the winter everything seemed to close up again, and the cold forced me to play chiefly before the fire in my mother's bedroom or behind the stove in the always warm kitchen.

Until I was in grammar school, we, unlike some of our more modern neighbors, did not have indoor plumbing or electric lights. Since the town had not yet acquired its own water system, to have running water we should have had to have a windmill. Our next-door neighbor did have one; and it was, I had to admit, an intriguing thing, both in the spectacle of its revolving blades in the daytime and in the mysterious, though comforting, soft gang-gang sound that it made during the night—always seeming to be talking to the wind about something. But we seemed not to miss indoor plumbing. On our enclosed back porch there was a fine pump with a sink, and there was a sink in the kitchen, and a stove capable of producing quantities of hot water. Next to my parents' room was a bathroom, really a dressing room, which, though without running water and the proper fixtures, could be used for my bath when the weather was warm. Otherwise, I had a tub in front of an open fire. Although according to a long-established custom, all-over baths at our house might have been confined to the ritual of Saturday nights, I am sure that no person or thing was allowed to go insufficiently washed.

So far as electric lighting was concerned, the little pallid bulbs in our neighbors' houses produced not a great deal more light than our lamps did, and they were not nearly so romantic. Always the lighting of the lamps in the evening was a pleasurable experience to me, though, as I learned, not necessarily to my mother, who particularly disliked the periodic chore of cleaning the globes and trimming the wicks. Hanging in the front hall was an impressively handsome lamp, with green glass base and shade and brass fixtures, that had to be lowered by a little chain before it could be lighted and drawn up again. This procedure was a special delight.

Outside the house were yards and outbuildings of various kinds that in our total fenced area (picket, paling, and wire fences being included) constituted a small family compound obviously designed for a certain amount of self-sufficiency. There was, for example, a wood yard surrounded by a high paling fence (usually white-washed) and dominated by the wood house (sometimes erroneously referred to as the smoke house), always smelling deliciously of freshly cut pine cord wood for the kitchen range or oak logs for the fireplaces. Here, too, were stored the garden tools, miscellaneous household gadgets too large for the broom closets inside our house, bags full of feed for the chickens, and even some large containers with household staples in them. At times the wood odor might be supplanted by the less enticing aroma of sauerkraut fermenting in a large earthen crock with a white plate and a clean rock on top; or even on occasion the smell of wine "working." These were great temptations to exploration and, especially in the event of wine, tasting—an act that several times produced remarkable and inexplicable hilarity among my playmates in the wood yard.

Next to this yard were the chicken yards: one stocked with laying hens and the other with pullets and other fowl destined for the pot or the frying pan. In a day when refrigeration was limited and quick-freezing unknown, the second yard was a constant and ready source of at least one type of meat. It was an axiom that a Southern woman who had on hand a pound cake, a baked ham, and a black silk dress was prepared to meet any occasion. A well-stocked chicken yard with a few eligible fryers or young baking hens already cooped up (for internal cleanliness, since my mother believed that no chicken should go directly from the ground to whatever cooking utensil was appropriate) served part of the same purpose. I remember vividly how the arrival of an unexpected guest always caused a hurried visit to the chicken coop, followed by a raucous wringing of necks and the odoriferous scalding of feathers at the sink on the back porch.

I must admit that I never watched any of this procedure if I could possibly avoid it, for the sight of blood and the entrails of chickens turned my stomach. I was very sensitive about eating chickens anyway, since I lived so close to them and knew them so intimately, having observed the mess that they could make of their yards. Thus the memory of anything nauseating about fowls might cause me suddenly to abstain. My mother liked to tell a story of how this squeamishness on my part almost broke up a company dinner.

It happened in this way:—In the spring chickens had a way of getting a disease that my father called the sore head. So he would get out some axle grease and a bottle of carbolic acid and make a paste which he applied to the heads of his pullets, most of which he had tamed and made friends of to such an extent that when they were in the best of health he only reluctantly allowed them to be slaughtered. After the application of his awful concoction, the chickens would stagger away looking grotesquely like masked creatures from outer space. I regarded this procedure, benevolent though it was, with particular nausea. Months after one of these spring rituals and all the chickens on the place were perfectly clean and sound came the day of a dinner party—probably a Sunday when a visiting minister and his wife were brought home from church. I was allowed to sit next to the guest of honor, who, when the chicken platter came around, said to me, "And what piece can I serve you, little man?" "None," I am alleged to have replied, and then airily, "I don't eat sore-headed chicken." At this point, my mother who rarely lost her composure was put to a strong test. After a brief stunned silence, she recovered sufficiently to explain that my remark had arisen out of an inordinately long memory. She was so embarrassed that she remembered nothing else about the meal, not even whether I got a stout switching after the guests left—which I in all probability did.

Whatever their function by day, the chicken yards often produced suspenseful nighttime experiences when the household would be aroused by such squawking as would raise the dead. What was it—a dog, a rat, a fox, a 'possum, or a two-legged marauder (usually expected to be black) who needed a meal? My father, who must have hunted when he was younger but who in my childhood never seemed to have a gun in the house, would regularly rush out onto the back porch and shout into the night. My mother could be counted on to be pulling him by the tail of his nightshirt and exhorting him to go no step farther. Chickens could be replaced but my father couldn't, and my mother believed in taking no chances with the unknown thing out there in the dark.

Beyond the chicken yards were the barn and that ingratiating but not always inviting creature, the cow—Bossy, as she was usually referred to with little originality. I was not allowed to go near her often. But when the milking woman failed to come in the evening, my father let me at times go with him to watch the amazing procedure as he milked. The sweet smell of the cow's breath and the taste of foamy warm milk right from the source are enduring memories, as are also the rows of earthen bowls of the white liquid that gathered thick layers of orange-yellow cream on our cool back porch. But I observed that Bossy could sometimes switch her ever-moving tail a little too vigorously at an errant fly or otherwise make a sudden kicking movement that would overturn the pail and fill the ground all around with a snow-white froth. This act was plainly not appreciated by my father, for he usually unloosed some mild expletives on the occasion.

Milk we had in great quantities: sweet milk, butter milk, and clabber. The last named was, of course, not drunk but eaten as a delicacy when it was sprinkled with sugar and grated nutmeg. Milk we had to cook with and even to sell. My mother had a few select customers who sent over their pitchers, knowing that what they paid for as a quart (ten cents, I think it was) would turn out to be nearly a half-gallon. But there were times in the spring that all the milk had to be poured out. The reason was that Bossy would eat wild onions that sprang up overnight in the pasture or the little yellow daisy-like flowers that used to come up in profusion no matter what one did to prevent their appearance. A trace of onion flavor would make the milk unpalatable, and so would the bitterness from the daisies.

Cows came and went, though since they were all named the same I could not tell them apart; and I was never told exactly what became of them when they left us. One cow I do remember with regret. This unlucky creature broke out of the barn into a field of something vastly worse than wild onions or daisies—namely, young millet; and through a night of gormandizing she got herself out of this world. My father discovered her the next morning, dead and horribly bloated, in the millet field. By a most unfortunate chance I got a glimpse of the carcass. As fate would have it, we had guests again—overnight ones this time—and my mother had prepared what she considered an elegant breakfast: steak and waffles. I remember the occasion well and the fact that I confined myself to waffles—in silence this time. I apparently had learned a little about what to say and what not to say at the table, just as I had intuitively sensed that some of our cows had previously gone to the abattoir to return to us finally as steaks. This last one would not, I hoped; but I was not then in a mood to take chances.

We had no horses, though horses and buggies were almost standard for the neighborhood. My parents had naturally had horses on the farm in the country, but they had brought none to town. I am sure that if my mother had thought it wise to have a horse and buggy, we should have had one. But as a consistently practical person given to few of the vanities, she felt that she had moved to town to be within walking distance of most of the objects of her interest: the church, the stores downtown, the houses of the neighbors that she wished to visit. If she happened to be invited to a place beyond walking range, her usual reply was that she would be glad to accept provided that she could "arrange a conveyance." This phrase she considered to be the proper wording. It simply meant the horse and buggy that Mr. Shealey could occasionally provide from his livery stable just diagonally across from the depot. Buggy rides that some of our neighbors took on Sundays on dusty, unpaved roads or ostentatiously around the town for the purpose of bowing to people resting sedately on their piazzas could be of no possible interest to my mother. They were to me, however; and I thrilled when one of my playmates asked me to go on a family buggy ride.

As one would expect, we had a large vegetable garden, full of spring and summer richness, with almost every green thing in it that grew in the region: beans of all sorts, potatoes, varieties of squash, cabbage, turnips, cantaloupes, watermelons, and so on, not to mention herbs like mint, sage, and dill. On the edges were some peach and pecan trees, and two or three enormous fig trees that in midsummer produced as many June bugs as figs. These insects could be as appealing to a child as fireflies, though maybe not quite so wonderful. For in spite of their disagreeable smell ("You smell like a June bug" was a crude expression of disapprobation for somebody who needed a bath), they could have strings attached to their legs and be tossed into the air to fly in circles around their captors. This evidence of childhood savagery is not pleasant to report, and in retrospect I have some feelings of guilt about it. The eighteenth-century poet, William Cowper, once wrote:

> I would not enter on my list of friends,
> (Though graced with polish'd manner and fine sense,
> Yet wanting sensibility), the man
> Who needlessly sets foot upon a worm.

In the light of this statement of universal benevolence, I regret that I was ever so unworthy; and I can only hope that this and other sensitive poets who have attributed to small living things without central nervous systems a capability of feeling pain comparable to that of human beings were more benevolent than scientific.

At the back of the vegetable garden in a little corner all its own was a small structure whose grayed clapboard siding would have tended to make it nearly invisible, even though it had not been surrounded by trellised vines and, in the spring and summer, by clumps of brownish-orange day lilies, the kind that also grew along the railroad tracks. This was, of course, the garden house (it could not in my family be referred to as anything else), and it took care of appropriate physical functions in as unobtrusive and modest a way as possible. Inside plumbing, when it came, made modesty in this manner ever so much simpler in most instances. A building so far outside a place of residence naturally exposed people to observation as they went back and forth—or so it might be expected to do. Thus one part of the magic of the time (if I may report from my rather immature powers of observation) was the way in which ladies somehow managed to be translated from dwelling house to garden house and back again without ever materializing in the outside air.

In this mini-tour of the "grounds," the side yards should not be completely neglected. Here, in beds that my mother would have liked to make off-limits to small boys, flowers were almost always in bloom: daffodils and other bulbs in the spring, roses and shasta daisies in the summer, chrysanthemums and golden-glow in the fall. I could not list them all even if I knew the names, for a fairly small space a ridiculous variety of plants thrived under the green thumb of the resident gardener.

In the front yard the two large magnolias were rich

in glossy, dark green leaves; and their great pallid blossoms spilling a rich sweetness on a late spring or early summer evening created an ineffable necromancy. But they all but precluded other flowers or grass. This fact constantly bothered my mother, who was unimpressed by magnolias, since they were no novelty to her and since she was incapable of appreciating what joy they could bring to small boys. Moreover, she felt that a mowable lawn was a necessary adjunct to a respectable town residence.

As I grew up, I was able to know both the advantages and the disadvantages of the trees. Climbing in a great magnolia could be an almost inexhaustible adventure. The branches were thick enough to make movement easy among them, and the shade was such as to render areas of the tree cool and private. There were splendid opportunities for "play-hiding" or genuine escape from problems involved in the world below and around the tree. My friends and I built "houses" and "offices" in the branches, hoisting up food and other types of supplies with crude little pulleys and communicating fictively from branch and tree to tree over yards and yards of wrapping twine to which empty tin cans were attached—our "telephones."

But then there came a day when I was reminded that possession (or at least occupancy) entailed responsibility—and that such responsibility involved raking leaves. As most people may know, a magnolia is not called a deciduous tree, for the term is usually applied to the kind of tree that loses its leaves in the fall and grows them back in the spring. But in the root-meaning of the word as simply "falling off," the magnolia is what I would call a permanently deciduous tree, for it sheds its leaves at all seasons.

So on selected Saturday mornings throughout the year, I might count on being provided with a rake and a split basket. And away I worked, not infrequently grumbling as I did so. My labor, it is true, did not go completely unrewarded, for I regularly collected a dime at the end of the job, however long it happened to take. Just as regularly on the same afternoon, I laid the dime on the shelf of the ticket window at the Ideal or Pastime Theater, whatever the name happened to be at the moment, for a ticket to several hours of pleasure with "The Perils of Pauline," "The Million Dollar Mystery," "The Red Circle," or another of a seemingly endless chain of exciting serials.

But as time went on, I became immensely bored with the periodic Saturday routine (though never by the movies), and I found opportunity for a nefarious teaming up with my mother in making a proposition to my father that he have the magnolias cut down. However he may have felt privately about the matter, the double pressure was too much to resist. So one fine morning several men appeared with saws, and down the trees came. My mother got her lawn; and I got freedom from raking leaves.—I mowed the lawn! So in the end I may have gained precious little.

What I lost it took me some years to realize fully. Even now I think at times of the enormity of my crime, and I am mildly haunted by the ghosts of two magnolia trees.

So much for the concomitants of the place. There were people, too.

Doing odd jobs about the house, sometimes cleaning lamps or plowing in the garden, was Cal, whom I appropriated as a supplement to Leila as a friend, playmate, and defender. Since Cal did not come every day but turned up only every now and then, I have a notion that he had a steady job on my father's acreage just outside the town limits which included, along with woods and an arable tract planted in cotton, four magnificent acres of pecan trees that occasioned a picnic period of nut gathering in the fall. The picture of Cal that I have retained is not always clear, but I remember him as having a mouth full of very white teeth, revealed by a constant smile, and as speaking with a soft musical drawl. One incident alone stands out as an example of my relationship with him, and that memory is due at least in part to the prompting of my mother. It occurred on a day when I was only slightly over four and when my mother, observing the rapid approach of a rain cloud, called Cal away from clipping the hedge and asked him to round me up and bring me inside the house. As he approached the back porch with me in his arms, he remarked to my mother in support of her apprehension, "Yes, m'am, it's already drapping rain." "You mustn't say drapping, Cal," I corrected him. "You must say dropping"—though I am sure we both left off the final g's. Whether or not this was an admirable evidence of precocity or whether it augured well for a teaching career is a moot point. Many scientific grammarians of a later day have said that ethnic linguistic patterns should not be tampered with. Maybe the best thing that can be said for this little pedagogue was that he was already a small pedant.

Another black man of a different sort that I saw from time to time with both interest and wonder was a most ancient peg-legged man who came now and then for packages of food and clothing and a little money that my mother always managed to find for him. I was taught to call him Uncle Jonathan, and he would explain in his gentle toothless way that he "belonged" to my mother. This relationship puzzled me no end until I was old enough to discover that he was the last survivor of my maternal grandfather's small group of slaves and that he lived in a cabin on the farm of one of my uncles.

Other relationships puzzled me, too. Though my

mother, with her inherited German notions of thrift and cleanliness, departed from the local custom of always having a black cook, there were two black women who appeared periodically to assist with some aspect of the housework. Dittie, who had big, forlorn eyes but always a sweet expression on her face, came every Monday to pick up the laundry ("washing" is the right word) and brought it back gleaming white and smelling of a kind of pine-smoke cleanliness on Friday afternoon or early Saturday morning. Ginsy, a proud and brusque creature turned up at any time she pleased, grabbed a broom or mop (sometimes without the slightest greeting) and started on a whirlwind cleaning spree that ultimately left greater disorder than order. She could always count on leaving our house with a mixed array of clothing, food, and bric-a-brac—in fact, anything as my mother complained that was not nailed or screwed down. The thing that I could not understand about both these women was that they called each other "Mrs. Barclay"— at least when they were joking together. That was my mother's name; and how could they have it, too, being black as they were? Again, the explanation given me was that both women were married to sons of slaves of my paternal grandparents. I still did not understand very well. The whole idea of slavery was completely incomprehensible.

As I grew older, it is true, Ginsy took it upon herself to educate me in the injustices and indignities suffered by her race for a century and more. As I look back, I can see her as an intelligent and genuine forerunner of the "freedom fighters" of the mid-century—an unlettered precursor of James Baldwin and The Fire Next Time. "Y'all white folks better look out," she would say. "You throw us niggers into jail and you cheats us in your stores. But it ain't gonna be like this forever. Another day is coming. Just you wait and see. Yes, sir, things is going to be different." I hadn't thrown any blacks into jail and I hadn't cheated any. But when the fire flew from Ginsy's eyes, I almost felt that I had; and I had vivid premonitions of the wrath to come. At the same time, I felt that Ginsy was a friend who would save me from the burning; and I enjoyed hearing her tell about her successful children: for example, Gladys, a handsome and virile youth in spite of his name, who was a chauffeur and mechanic; and Marie, a daughter who glittered with all sorts of clothing and jewelry when she came home from New York where she worked—doing what, Ginsy never said.

So much for the people who came in and out of the house as "help" of one sort or another, without being remotely similar to a staff. The feudal implications ironically there were thin, indeed. These were simply people that my mother employed or endured—and in either case gently; for regardless of her strong will and determined notions, not to mention her frequent grumbling, she had great sensitivity for the feelings of people and especially of the blacks. I remember well that both my parents gave me almost formal little lectures about etiquette in regard to them. For example, Ginsy could say "nigger," but I could not under any circumstances. Had I done so I would have been punished with the same rapidity and severity that I would have been had I used a profanity or an obscenity. I would have been carefully trained to say Negro as dictionaries give the pronunciation if my local dialect had admitted long "o's" at the ends of words. It didn't. Therefore, I always pronounced words like window, pillow, and follow as if they ended in a "schwa" or a short "a." So far as the final sound was concerned, Negro obviously fell in the same category. To people who speak the general American dialect, a pronunciation like "Negra" has been considered contemptuous.

Nothing could be farther from the truth in our case. We were simply doing the best we could.

In other matters, too, I was taught to be courteous and considerate in all ways to people of different races and colors, especially the elderly ones—whom I, following the regional custom, had always to address as "Uncle" or "Aunt" according to sex. I must admit that this custom was another thing that did not make sense to me, but neither did "manners" in general always do so.

If to my earliest age there were sources of puzzlement and wonder in people, there were also sources in things—so many in fact that to enumerate them would only be boring. I need hardly mention the way in which light could come on without having a match struck to it, or the big box on the wall that seemed to have a little woman or man in it who would talk to you if you turned the crank and put a black thing to your ear, or, as a closely related wonder, the little people in the wooden boxes on hall tables who sang to you or produced instrumental music through a morning-glory horn. There were sources of terror, too, and these were bigger and far more intangible. I hardly need mention fear of the dark, most horrible when for misbehavior I was sentenced to the most uncivilized of all punishment: that of being locked up in a dark clothes closet. Beyond this fear, by far the most dramatic ones were those of thunderstorms and fires—both of which I acquired, to my everlasting sorrow, from my mother, God rest her soul. ("Why, Son," she is saying somewhere up there, "you know this is not true!")

With the first audible rumble of thunder in the summertime, I was most often called immediately from play into the house, where my mother herded me along with anybody else who might be around into the parlor (the occasion was too solemn for the hall sitting area), drew and closed the green blinds, pulled down the shades, and required whoever had been gathered together to remain in prayerful silence until she pronounced some sort of *"nunc dimittis servum tuum, Domine"*—though her Protestant soul would wince at my calling it that. Jonathan Edwards, I believe, explained how he conquered his own fear of storms in the discovery that thunder was the voice of God; and thus his terror was transformed into religious acceptance and assurance. I wish that I had been able to achieve the same attitude. I could easily have been convinced of God's presence in the elements, but I could derive no comfort from any kind of assessment that His voice, though admonitory, was chiefly benevolent. So when the lightning crackled and boomed outside, my terror produced a barely controlled hysteria. I bit my lips, cried gently, and prayed fervently to be spared the wrath of an angry God, the Old Testament one who was obviously displaying His fire and brimstone.

My mother's terror I could not well determine. I was too busy with my own. All I could see was that she was sitting stolidly and silently in the semi-darkness. When my father was at home, he, it is true, managed to escape the parlor seance. He was completely unafraid of the storm, and he liked to watch its progress from the front or back porch. Such bravery, however, only served to increase my apprehension. It seemed too much of a gamble with heavenly anger, and I trembled at the thought of my father's possibly being struck down.

Fires during the daytime were frightening enough, but when they occurred at night they were something especially eerie and horrendous. In the first place, the alarm was sounded by blasts of a whistle at the cotton mill on the edge of town whose blood-curdling note would have made a banshee wail sound like the cooing of a turtle dove by comparison. At the blasts (indicating by the number the endangered area) the whole town was galvanized into action; and everybody went, following the billowing smoke in the daytime or the red glare in the sky at night and taking along babies in arms and other children as if to a circus or carnival. As I look back, I can remember the comic aspects—the motley appearance of the hastily dressed spectators, the breathless, late arrival of the volunteer fire company, pulling a cart with a hose reel on it, fumbling with the hydrant when there was one, and eventually getting more water on themselves than on the fire. But at the time, I could see nothing amusing about the situation. Most houses, in the days before we had efficient fire engines, were burned all the way down, unless a daytime roof blaze was involved that could be doused by a bucket brigade and a few daring young climbers; and I could think of nothing more pitiful than a yard full of furniture and clothing lit by the light of a burning house. Nor could I bear the next day to look at the gaunt chimneys standing amid the ruins.

I can recall in exact detail many of the fires that I saw. One especially terrifying night stands out when, with my eyes stuck shut by conjunctivitis, I could in my blindness only hear the alarm and sense the feverish activity in the household. Then there was one horrible Sunday when I had gone home with Aunt Allie to have the midday meal in her apartment. As we were just beginning to eat, the alarm sounded. Rushing to a window, we saw an enormous cloud of smoke billowing up in the general direction of the street on which I lived. Plainly, a few blocks beyond, the town's large cotton-seed oil mill with its several storage tanks was ablaze, the inferno being easily visible. Up my aunt snatched me by the hand and away we went, with me half running and half flying through the air until we reached home, thoroughly breathless. Large burning flakes were falling everywhere from the sky. My father had put a ladder up to the roof, and he was briskly pumping water from the back porch pump for a small bucket brigade trying to keep the shingles wet on the main house and the outhouses. It was a narrow escape, and it seemed hours before the big fire died down and the danger was over. I can't remember at all what my mother was doing at the time. Maybe she was sitting in the quiet somewhere, maybe again in the parlor, asking God to spare us. I suggest the parlor as the place, for here it seemed most respectful to address the Deity, as in times of thunder storms. I am sure that I was praying just as hard under a smoky sky. If I tended to invoke the God of fire and brimstone in heavy weather, I doubtless prayed to the same one in times of holocaust. My iconography is traceable not only to the prints in our copy of *Pilgrim's Progress* but also the numerous little color-printed cards that I brought home from Sunday School. There was a vivid one of Moses coming down with those two white things that looked like tombstones from his talk with God on Mt. Sinai, the latter engulfed in fire. There was another one with the picture of a great angel (I had not then read the Bible story carefully and I was a long way away from Milton; so I thought he was God) with wings aloft and with a stern finger pointing the way for a cowering Adam to get out of Eden.

But our prayers had been answered, and I had not been ejected from Eden. At the same time, I needed further assurance; so I begged to be allowed to sleep with my parents that night.

III

COUNTRY STORE

IRONICALLY, the contemporary drugstore that sells almost everything is the lineal descendant of the old country store. But, with its fluorescent glare and its tasteless and aseptic systematization, it has none of the romantic qualities of its ancestor. Examples of the genuine item still exist, to be sure, in whatever small towns and remote regions remain; and imitations to ensnare the tourist trade are to be nauseatingly encountered in various places. But along with the disappearance of the small independent operation in a nation smitten with megalomania, monopolies, shopping malls, and supermarkets, the true country store (one that evokes something other than trumped-up nostalgia) is going the way of the whooping crane.

My father's store was in many respects the real thing, though it was a shade more sophisticated than the ones that might have been found at the cross-roads; moreover, under the care of the junior partner, my aunt, it had an orderliness rarely to be expected in such an establishment. To me it was a kind of second home and a place of endless opportunity and fascination, not to mention an area of freedom and indulgence away from my mother's sharp eyes and strict discipline.

In the 1902 special edition of the *Advocate* the wide scope of my father's offerings was indicated, along with emphasis on the agency for farm equipment. In the 1917 town directory, on the other hand, the main focus of the ad is on Star-Brand shoes, suggesting that the store might have become far more limited in its custom. Such was not the case, for it still seemed to supply everything—or almost everything.

A photograph surviving from the time of the directory shows the front as being architecturally classic (though this may be a funny word to apply to it), with four small fluted iron columns topped by slightly ornamented capitals, marking off two long display windows from a set-in entrance with double doors. One window displays shoes over a large outside sign bearing a red star and the legend: "Star Brand Shoes Are Better." The other window contains china and crystal. A panel on each side is neatly lettered with the name of the firm. On the broad cement sidewalk, marked off in squares, is a plow from the handle of which hangs a horse collar nonchalantly. An almost depleted bunch of bananas (fly-specked, I fear) is suspended pathetically from a wire attached to the ceiling left of the entrance.

The decidedly *dégagée* appearance of the whole scene, as well as that of my father and aunt standing outside as proprietors, suggests that they were caught in an unguarded moment by an itinerant photographer who was simply going down the block on a summer's day picking up a few dollars wherever he could. My father has on a straw hat, a white shirt with a black string tie, a vest, but no jacket. My aunt looks far more drab and shapeless than I ever remember her. Plainly no preparation or posing was involved; and the best that can be said about the photograph is that it is a genre work or an example of *"l'art déshabillé"*—both terms being pretentious disguises for the way the scene is pictured: that is, disgracefully. There is small wonder that the photograph was well hidden away until I had the brashness to dig it out.

So much for the outside of the store. Inside, it seemed to my eyes cavernous. It was over a hundred feet long; and since windows were provided only at the front and back, it was something less than bright even on the brightest days. Artificial lighting was achieved by two long rows of sockets with naked bulbs hanging from the ceiling. These were both of limited efficiency and utility. In the early days of the store, electricity was available only from six or seven o'clock to ten o'clock in the evening. Thus the weak, reddish glow from the carbon filamented globes could actually be observed only on Saturday nights when the store stayed open until nine and when, even then, the electric lights might be supplemented with oil lamps.

To the left of the entrance to the store were two glass show-cases containing candy. Understandably this fact is clearly etched in my memory, for the cases formed a great treasure house to which I was admitted with some freedom so long as I was not greedy or indiscreet. (Unlike other children that I knew, I did not have to come in with a penny clutched in a grubby fist.)

Then came the large shoe department, about which my father cared most and I cared least. Across the way my aunt presided over an even larger area with shelves, tables, stands, and glass showcases that held piece goods, notions, hats and ribbons of all sorts— meaningless objects to me. The spacious central area contained tables and stands holding china and glass forward, with kitchen utensils aft; and beyond came an assortment of hardware items. Toys were in the forward central area, too, in the Christmas season. At the back of the store was the grocery department.

In this area I remember chiefly the large aromatic wheel of American cheese ("rat cheese" to the trade), equipped with a cutting device and housed under a round wooden cover near a barrel of round, fluted sweet crackers. A slice of cheese between two of these crackers, I observed, frequently provided customers in the store a quick lunch or afternoon snack, washed down with a soft drink at room temperature. (There was no cooler, except perhaps in the middle of the summer. Iced drinks were available chiefly at the two drug stores.)

Two such unlikely companions as a barrel of molasses and a drum of kerosene stood not very far apart: the first for customers who came with their own earthen jug or glass containers and the second for those who brought in their own little oil cans whose spouts were frequently stoppered with a small Irish potato. The molasses barrel was a nuisance, for the tap often spilled a sticky mess on the floor that drew flies—anathema to both proprietors of the store.

Several kinds of canned vegetables were on the shelves, together with a variety of other staples. But there were no green vegetables in stock. Fruits there were, on the other hand, in season: apples, oranges, bananas, not to mention nuts of several sorts and raisins.

During school days I had little time to spend at the store. But Saturdays were another matter. These were gala days when the roads into town were clouded with dust from the wagons and buggies of country folk coming in to do their week's shopping, and the streets were filled from early morning until closing time at night. My father always hired extra help for Saturdays, but he always seemed to be able to give personal attention to customers of long standing for whom he provided hitching facilities in a lot to the rear of the store and cane-bottomed chairs on the pavement in front. In the winter, of course, the chairs were grouped, as tradition demanded, around the only source of heat in the store: a large pot-bellied stove near the grocery department—and the cracker barrel. (Here a cliché is unavoidable.)

Outside, a carnival atmosphere prevailed with people sitting on chairs and benches or milling about, talking and laughing and smoking pipes. At times, too, they ate fried fish (smelling wonderful) between thick slices of bread obtained from a little shack on a back street called a restaurant and operated by an expert Negro cook. Like the English fish and chips this food could be transported in the hands through the use of a rough newspaper cornucopia and eaten among friends on the sidewalk—a fact that gave several areas the effect of rustic sidewalk cafes.

Most of the time the noise of the croud was moderate, but it was occasionally raucous. A drunk or two could often be counted on to add amusement and excitement—the latter of which always produced Mr. Darby, the constable, who was a tall, dour but not unpleasant man, wearing a dark suit and a broad-brimmed black hat, and sporting a pistol in a belt beneath the skirts of his coat. I always liked him, regarding him as small boys have later regarded Gary Cooper or John Wayne. And this was in spite of the fact that both of my parents at times told me that, if I misbehaved, Mr. Darby would "get" me and put me in the "calaboose"—which was on a side street barely a block from the main business district. The calaboose I had from time to time slipped away to inspect, concluding that the forbiddingly ugly little unpainted wooden building was not a place where I ever wanted to be, for I had seen sad and often menacing faces with bad teeth and red-rimmed eyes peering out of the little barred windows. Some of the faces were white, but most were black. A particular memory is that of a disheveled black woman who thrust a gnarled fist through the bars, saying, "Here, kid, take this nickel and get me a bag of ground peas and goobers." "You mean peanuts?" I said, not entirely certain what she meant—but guessing correctly. Then overcome by fear and cowardice, I turned away and ran as fast as I could back to the store.— I knew the stench of the jailhouse also, and I had seen the straw and the dirty old blankets on the floor. For me I needed no better deterrent to misbehavior. But I was quite sure that I was on the good side of Mr. Darby and that he would not put me there, or even do anything quite so bad as something my mother did: namely, put me in a dark closet when I became recalcitrant.

However exciting Saturdays might have been, there was nothing quite so splendid as the day in October when there came a great opening of packing boxes of Christmas merchandise in the back of the store. Regularly I sought a lofty perch of some sort from which I could swoop down like a bird of prey on a toy or some other object that appealed to me so that I could make a claim on it before it got to the shelves. My father's indulgence worked in so many instances that I never went away greatly disappointed. Moreover, the things I wanted that had not turned up among the Christmas merchandise I knew quite well how to get. In my father's office, fenced off from the rest of the store by a lattice, was a reasonably thick catalogue of a wholesale place called the Baltimore Bargain House, with all kinds of things in it like Indian suits and cowboy outfits and trains and magic lanterns or even small toy moving-picture projectors. My only necessary procedure was to draw a circle around a desired object and leave the catalogue open at the right page on the desk at which my father stood to do his bookkeeping. After a few weeks of suspenseful waiting, the object usually turned up.

There was one disadvantage in this kind of bounty and indulgence—if disadvantage, indeed, it really was. For a child who had everything already and well in advance, Christmas could have little glamor or surprise. Just to be like the other children, I hung up my stocking.

And Santa Claus came; but in addition to the candy, raisins, oranges, apples, and nuts that he brought me (all of which were easily available in the store anyway), he brought me only such boring things as gloves and stockings and caps. When little boys whispered to me that Santa Claus was really my father, I was far too blasé to be disillusioned, distressed, or amused. Ho hum, I had known the real Santa Claus for some time, and he suited me perfectly.

Another of my father's indulgences to me during the Christmas season—at least, when I had reached the maturity of seven or eight years—was to let me play at being a merchant myself. So when the weather was good, a packing box was arranged on the sidewalk from which I was allowed to sell firecrackers, sparklers, and roman candles, along with packaged candies, chewing gum, and other small items. I am not sure whether this privilege was due to my father's desire to begin my training in business early, or whether he merely wanted to get me out from under his feet in the rush season. I strongly suspect that the latter reason is the most likely. As for my merchandising career, it was for the most part successful; but I have to admit to one serious misstep that brought down my father's wrath on me. One day I quietly emptied my till into a pocket, went over to a rival store, and bought a red train—the wind-up kind. Almost everything about the act, as I was soon to discover, was wrong. I will not go into the specific sins that it included, but my father detailed them to me clearly; and most of them were scripturally referenced. And least of all was the little matter of disloyalty to our own business interests. At any rate, I sheepishly took the train back. And never again did any money go from the till to my pocket until my father had audited my account and given me my daily commission. Good business was always to him honest business, and it was not too early at my age to have that fact engraved on my cranium. I often had a chance to watch how he himself operated in selling. His measuring cups were always filled to overflowing. His pounds were never short. He never tried to palm off shoddy merchandise. My father's marking code (the usual ten non-repeating letters representing numerals from 1 to 10) was "Of Industry." (How mature I felt when this secret was entrusted to me!) This well summarized his simple old-fashioned philosophy of work and getting ahead. A passage from Deuteronomy (25:13-15) was his guide to business conduct:

> You shall not have in your bag two kinds of weights, a large and a small. You shall not have in your house two kinds of measures, a large and a small. A full and just weight you shall have; that your days may be prolonged in the land which the Lord your God gives you.

My mother had another biblical quotation about how your measure should be filled to overflowing when, as I have mentioned already, she sold milk all the year to our neighbors, or daffodils in the spring, or vegetables in the summer, or nuts in the fall.

Merchandising in a small town such as ours was, when I was first able to observe it, still partially on the level of bartering. Country people still brought in eggs, cured hams, corn, and other farm products to exchange for manufactured items and commodities that they themselves did not produce. (The folk expression used as a stock reply to an overcurious interest in how a person acquired such and such a thing was "I stole eggs and bought it"—an indication of the importance of one primitive type of trading.) I listened with fascination to the kind of bargaining that went on between my father and his customers, especially if the total purchase was considerable. And I always waited for the final question from the purchaser: "Now what you gonna throw in?"

"Lagniappe" was the word a good deal farther south and west. "Boot" it might have been with us. But the meaning was the same. And I observed that my father seemed to be able to meet the situation with both generosity and some shrewdness.

Thrift, industry, and honesty are fine things I learned, but even the best things are subject to misinterpretation. And because we did not live beyond our means as some of our neighbors did, my father was thought by some people to be close-fisted or tight or stingy. This fact was brought to me through the peculiar cruelty of children who, undoubtedly reflecting what they had picked up from their elders, said to me taunting things like "Your papa is so stingy that he jumps over the fence to keep from wearing out the gate hinges" or "Your father chased a fly around the block because it had stolen a grain of sugar from his store." Since I knew better, I was not greatly bothered. Even at a relatively early age I was able to sense the fact that unlike some other merchants in town he had never taken shelter in a bankruptcy, or suddenly one night "sold his business to the Yankees" (as the expression went for those who profited from a fortuitous fire covered by a generous insurance policy with a Northern company), or misappropriated the funds of people who had given them money to "keep" or invest for them. Every now and then I heard of men who cut their throats in the cow barn or hanged themselves in the attic or took bichloride or mercury tablets "by mistake" when they had overspent and overgambled. Nothing like that could happen to my father, for I knew that he neither "splurged" nor gambled. Once he confessed to me that he had bought some cotton futures—a favorite form of gambling, I later learned, of many of the business men down town. (I couldn't quite understand what "buying futures" was other than going over to the telegraph office in the depot, writing down figures on a piece of yellow paper, and then later getting another piece of yellow paper with figures on it in return.) At any rate, after my father had played the game for a week or so and lost and won a few dollars, he decided to get out; and get out he did for good. So far as his business was concerned, though he extended credit to a great many of his customers, he conducted his own affairs on a strictly cash basis. This kind of conduct was so extraordinary that it made sense to very few people. Moderate success and a clear conscience were all my father aimed for. And these are what he got. *Requiescat in pace!*

One final note should not be omitted. The downtown merchants had all agreed to a week-day closing time of six o'clock and a Saturday closing at nine. To signal the fact Mr. Eugene Collins, who had a store carrying groceries and school books just a few doors down from my father, appeared with a long, battered brass horn and blew a mighty blast. He might have been Joshua under the walls of Jericho, or Childe Roland under the Dark Tower, or Gabriel winding that final blast, for all the enthusiasm and might that he put into it. In the dark of a winter day or the brightness of a summer one, it was always strange and thrilling. In our place there was at the signal much banging of the rear fire doors, as well as much throwing of cloths over merchandise that needed to be covered for the night and much checking of safe and cash drawers. In the summertime especially, the front doors were locked with a sigh of relief.

On the way home there was ice to be picked up and carried on a string to our backporch, where it was chopped up to go into tall glasses of iced tea or into the churn where whipped cream, custard, and mashed peaches were waiting to be turned into ice cream. And

IV

THE DAY OF THE OCTOPUS

MY first vivid memory of Aunt Tessie goes back to one morning when my mother and I were looking through the slanted louvers of our drawn blinds down toward Trigman's Corner, so called after the people who lived there. The act was one of ritual. The train from the east arrived at 8:30, and the mellow sound of its approaching whistle was a signal for an expectant pause in the life of all Bayesville as a sort of invocation to the day. Everything waited for the train from Columbia. It brought money in manila packages to start the daily routine of the bank; and it disgorged merchandise for the stores: crates of celery and early string beans from Florida and cardboard boxes of fancy millinery from New York. It brought the morning paper and the mail, with good news and bad. It brought natives returning from long journeys. It brought drummers and visitors. We always watched it go by with a combination of awed silence and vibrant thrill. After it had huffed past, doggedly overcoming the inertia that it had acquired from its stop at the buttercup-yellow station a few blocks away, we still looked toward Trigman's Corner to see whether it had brought anybody to our neighborhood.

This morning I saw nothing until my mother caught up her checked gingham apron in a gesture of panic and exclaimed, "My Lord, there's Tessie!" She then disappeared on some frantic mission into another part of the house, leaving the window to me.

By this time Aunt Tessie had passed the corner and had walked into a shaft of brilliant sunlight. I remember quite indelibly that she wore a full, long green skirt drawn tightly in the middle of her body by a dark belt. Above it floated a rough sphere of purplish waist and a hat that erupted plumes of a dark rich brown. Somewhat incongruously, I thought, an overfilled net bag was flopping alongside.

I hasten to say that distance always had much to do with any enchantment that Aunt Tessie might have induced. Viewed more closely, her skirt and hat were likely to appear frowzy and her waist, soiled. Moreover, the pasty, almost featureless plainness of her face was always severely emphasized by the minor tumult of her blondined hair and the haphazard application of make-up. Powder was caked in the creases, and face and lip rouge were applied as if she had put them on just before having been routed out by a midnight fire.

Cosmetics too obviously displayed were always hard for my family to take. Badly put on they were insupportable.

Aunt Allie had often said confidentially to my mother, "Tessie is just a plain mess, a plain mess." My mother, who had strong and sometimes curious notions of propriety, accepted the opinion without approving the language. She always regarded the word "mess" as furiously indelicate; and even thought she thought it described quite accurately the florid bunch of indelicacies that Aunt Tessie so plainly was, she flinched at the sound.

Now that Aunt Tessie was descending upon us the question was a less academic one. From my mother's flight I could sense merely that confusion had struck the household. Nevertheless, with the brash confidence of my six years, I ran to the piazza to confront the newcomer. Whether my going to meet an assumed menace was a gesture of defending my mother or whether it was purely a matter of curiosity, I do not know. Nor am I certain that some of the motivation might not have involved an instinctive recognition of the basic rites of courtesy and of the necessity for performing them regardless of consequences.

Anyway, I promptly regretted my brashness when Aunt Tessie caught me up to her, engulfing me like a morass. At this stage of my life I had only two classifications for female relatives: wet kissers and dry kissers. Most female relatives were repulsive enough, but wet kissers were the worst. And Aunt Tessie was indubitably a wet kisser. I suddenly hated her and her wetness and the sickening miasma of sweetness and mustiness that hung about her. And I fought my way out of a dark tangle, closing my eyes and flailing my arms as I did so.

"Oh, my! Oh, little Paulie," said Aunt Tessie. (I hated being called Paulie. My name was Paul, Jr.) "That isn't a nice boy, is it? You don't act like a nice boy, and you don't love your Aunt Tessie. Your poor old Aunt Tessie. I'll bet you don't treat your Aunt Allie that way. I'll bet you love your Aunt Allie."

I didn't answer anything. I simply turned and ran, and I landed squarely in the middle of my mother who had by this time opened the screen door. The impact took her breath. As a result, she greeted her sister-in-law with an irresolution that she would have masked only a little better had she been in full control of her faculties.

Aunt Tessie had allowed herself no opportunity to question her welcome. She brushed my mother aside and marched straight through the front door and into the spare bedroom to deposit her net bag.

"Now!" she said when she returned to the hall,

unbuttoning her worn gloves. "Big Paul can get my valise from the depot this afternoon. Come, let's you and me and little Paulie sit down and talk a while.—No use going back to that kitchen, Emma. No use spending all your life in an old kitchen. You live only once, I always say; and if you're going to be cooked to death, it ought to be in another place. I always say to myself, Emma's just too good a housekeeper. She spends too much time cooking and sweeping and dusting. When she gets to heaven, she won't be happy unless she's got a broom in her hand, sweeping up those ivory palaces."

Cackling in what she intended to be genial expansiveness, she gathered both my mother and me and pushed us into the parlor—always darkly cool on account of the drawn blinds and always smelling faintly of furniture polish.

"I've got something on the stove!" said my mother, attempting to draw away, but succeeding only in being feckless before a possessive force.

"Oh, pshaw!" said Aunt Tessie, sniffing the air with authority. "Oh, pshaw! Paulie, you just run back and see if the snap beans are boiling over. Run along for your Aunt Tessie. Like a nice boy. Run along now."

Needing no further urging, I promptly did what I was told. In the kitchen everything was serene in the precise kind of order demanded by my mother, who insisted on doing her own housework and who would tolerate a Negro servant only occasionally. Nothing was giving off any odor or was in the slightest danger of boiling over.

When I had done my duty, I did not return to the parlor. I kept on going straight out of the house until I reached my most secure refuge, a seat in the mid-branches of one of our two large magnolia trees.

In appraisal of the new situation confronting us, I had quickly conceived of Aunt Tessie as the picture-book octopus with waving tentacles of blue-green jelly reaching out to absorb us all. I'd already divined that as long as she stayed in our house she'd be telling us what to do in every move we made, that she would comment on every mouthful of food we took, that we'd never go to bed at night or get up in the morning without finding Aunt Tessie under foot. And in my burning resentment, my present resolution was to stay in the tree—if necessary, to set up permanent residence there.

My father, of course, routed me out at our noon dinner hour. At the table his face was as grave as my mother's was frantic. Aunt Tessie was one of my father's unmarried sisters and she had just given up a job "clerking" in a store over in Stanton, I gathered. The suitability of such an occupation for her had been dubious to begin with, but anything that allowed Aunt Tessie to function on her own was better than having her on our hands.

"I don't see the point, Tessie," my father said. "You take a job; then you quit it. You're always changing jobs, changing jobs. How're you going to get anywhere? Answer me that? You can't always be changing jobs every time the moon changes."

"I'm a lady," Aunt Tessie replied, assuming a refined tone, "and I don't have to work—not with sweet brothers and sisters ready and willing to give me a home. And I intend to remain a lady. You know about that floorwalker at Brown and Chapman. You wouldn't have had your own sister stay there and be—'No, sir,' I said, 'I don't have to take insults from anybody. I'll go to Paul's. He'll be glad to have me—he and dear little Emma. I don't have to take freshness from anybody. No, sir.'— That's what I said."

"But," my father went on, "there's Clarina. She lives downtown in Stanton. Why couldn't you have gone to her until you could get another job? Stanton is a big city, full of department stores; or, far better, full of rich old women who need companions; and at Clarina's you'd have been right on the spot, ready for any opening."

"I went to Clarina's last time," said Aunt Tessie, "when I left 'notions' at Ardway's on account of that old buyer. And to tell the truth, I sort of felt that I had a rest coming to me—a kind of vacation, you know. So I just said to myself, 'Tessie, you go right on over to Paul's and Emma's. You won't be a bit of trouble. Just another plate to put on the table. That's all.—Mamma always said that Paul was one of the sweetest of her boys, so kind and big-hearted.'"

"You know you're always welcome, Tessie," said my father, forced to a little softness when Aunt Tessie pulled out the tremolo. "When I have a crust of bread to divide, I'll divide it with you. But—"

"There!" said Aunt Tessie. "There now, it's all settled. We don't have to say another word about an old job. Do we, Paul? Do we, Emma?"

That was certainly all there was to the argument. Dinner was now over. Aunt Tessie reached down into a pocket, pulled out a stick of chewing gum, peeled off the silver, folded the gum into a neat little roll, and popped it into her mouth. My mother was horrified. She considered that there was nothing more vulgar or even sinful than for a lady to chew gum. My own reaction was unfavorable for an entirely different reason. There was nothing that made my mouth water so much as a piece of "tutti-frutti"; and I had not been done the courtesy of being offered even half a stick.

"Doctor's orders," Aunt Tessie commented gratuitously. "One of the best aids to digestion.—We'll have to get you some chewing gum, Paulie, when we go down town to the drug store. We might get a cherry smash."

At that I'm afraid I stuck my hands over my face and

ran away from the table. The act was a very ugly one and I knew it. Somehow I was impelled to be mean and ugly against my will. I must have realized that my dilemma, like that of the rest of the family, would be a permanent one of trying to do my duty to Aunt Tessie while keeping my personal revulsion from making me act like a barbarian. At this point, however, a sterner outside influence stepped in. My father would not allow me to act with less control than he himself had.

"Paul, Jr.," he said in his sharpest voice. "Paul, Jr., come back at this moment. What do you say when you're spoken to? Have you forgotten how to be a gentleman?"

I came back.

"Thank you, Aunt Tessie," I said mechanically. "I would please like some tutti-frutti and a cherry smash at the drug store. Thank you very much.—May I go now please? May I go?"

Without really waiting for my father's nod, I fled. What a farce this whole thing was! What a farce! Of course, I wouldn't get the chewing gum or the soda at the drug store. Nobody was a bigger fraud than Aunt Tessie—with her promises!

And so there was a long, long year in which Aunt Tessie enveloped us and we had no life of our own. Surely enough, she told us when to go to bed and when to get up—or rather she repeated what she "said to herself" about getting healthy, wealthy, and wise, as if she were the only begetter of the stale maxims that she daily dispensed. She made our opinions for us, and she monopolized the conversation either when we had guests or when we didn't. If we had a call from Mrs. Trigman, whose daughter (much to the alarm of everybody) was separated from her husband, Aunt Tessie was sure to discourse on how terribly awful divorces were. And if it was Mrs. Ashworth, she was equally sure to make some reference to the sad story of the late Mr. Ashworth, who had cut his throat with a razor behind his barn. And once when Mr. Gaylord had had a fire in his store, Aunt Tessie remarked point-blank to his wife, "Charlie Gaylord knew the right time to sell to the Yankees, didn't he? Just when he had the place full of old junk he couldn't sell to anybody else."

In other ways, Aunt Tessie brought chaos to our house. She opened the blinds in the parlor and rearranged the furniture. She draped her raffish clothes all over the spare bedroom and she made our new bathroom a shambles. I was so ashamed of Aunt Tessie. I was sure that nobody else had such a tacky and vulgar relative as she. And to aggravate the situation, there was for all of us her engulfing affection—spongy and unwanted like herself.

Sometimes in spells of violence I fought her when she tried to help me with arithmetic exercises or when she dictated where, what, and with whom I should play. But I never really won a battle. I always ended in shame and remorse.

"There you go," Aunt Tessie would say. "What did I tell you? You love your Aunt Allie, but you don't love your poor old Aunt Tessie. One day you'll regret what you're doing to Aunt Tessie. You'll be sorry you haven't been a sweet boy always. Some day—"

When my father cleverly got Mr. Fairless to employ Aunt Tessie at the New York Racket Store, we felt that we had a partial reprieve. There were large parts of the day when my mother could call her house her own; and there were afternoons when I could play as I chose. But Aunt Tessie still framed our days with her presence in the early mornings and the evenings.

Then Mr. Van Hoek came. He was totally unexpected. Had he dropped entirely from the sky (with his unfamiliar name and his aloof manner) he could not have been more strange to us—or, as succeeding events proved, more welcome. One afternoon after store-closing time he simply came driving up with Aunt Tessie in a T-model Ford coupe whose rear compartment had been replaced by a platform holding a tarpaulin-covered affair that we could not at first identify.

Aunt Tessie hopped out gaily, waved the car off, and came into the house.

"I see that you have a new conveyance," said my mother, who attached some sort of elegance to the word "conveyance" and who was using it now for the double function of masking curiosity and expressing irony.

For once Aunt Tessie did not elaborate. She went straight to her room, singing one of her tantalizingly indistinguishable tunes sounding vaguely like "Smiles," both off pitch and off beat.

My mother, of course, told my father, and my father brought the matter up at the supper table.

"Who is your friend, Tessie?" he asked as archly as he knew how.

"Oh, pshaw," said Aunt Tessie, determined to keep her own counsel. "Oh, pshaw, he isn't anybody at all. Just a drummer I met. Mr. Whitacre introduced me— Well, he's just a friend."

"I seem to remember a floorwalker in Stanton," said my father, looking down at his plate. "Hadn't you better—mind?"

"Mr. Van Hoek's a gentleman," replied Aunt Tessie. "I can tell a gentleman when I see one."

"You ought to have asked him in," said my mother.

"Oh, pshaw, Emma," said Aunt Tessie, "he's just a chance acquaintance."

With the curse of precocity working at full speed, I immediately visualized the stranger as Aunt Tessie's beau and the very idea set me off into hysterical laughter. Aunt Tessie joined in and, in one of our rare moments of congeniality, we both laughed until tears streamed down our faces. For my behavior I was subsequently sent away from the table. Aunt Tessie, of course, could be outrageous with impunity.

The gentleman with the fancy name, we learned (though not immediately through Aunt Tessie), was a sewing machine salesman. And the peculiar contraption on the back of his Ford was a demonstrator. We did not get a good look at Mr. Van Hoek until a month or so later.

I remember coming in one afternoon from play and finding him with my mother and Aunt Tessie in the parlor. Aunt Tessie gathered me in with her usual mother-hen manner and introduced me in a far more orthodox way than I might have expected of her. Our guest was a rather stout middle-aged man who wore a snow-white shirt, a black string tie neatly tied, and a well-pressed dark suit. His face was round and reddish. A fringe of primly plastered yellowish-gray hair surrounded what I later discovered to be the bald top of his head, and he wore large, crisply trimmed mustachios of a color reasonably well matching his hair. His breathing was audibly asthmatic, and his voice sounded a little as if it were strained through cheese cloth. He spoke in a politely measured manner with an intonation and an accent that I judged to be foreign. A little jade monkey hung on a gold chain stretched across his comfortable stomach.

Anybody could see that he was everything that Aunt Tessie was not and that, exactly as she had insisted, he was a gentleman—even though he was a sort of caricature of one.

"Miss Tessie has told me what a fine lad you are, Sir," he said, addressing me as if I were quite grown. "She thinks you are a very proper young gentleman."

I blushed. This was rank extravagance. Aunt Tessie had little reason to think me a gentleman of any sort. I had run from her and had fought her and had done everything bad to her that I could think of. The pain of my conscience was considerable.

"He looks better," said my mother, "when his hands are washed and his hair brushed. Run along now, Paul, and clean yourself up."

I was so fascinated by Mr. Van Hoek, by the way he talked, and by the little monkey pendant on his stomach, that I hoped he would see only the blackness of my outside—not the ugliness that I concealed. I backed out of the room, not taking my eyes off him until I tumbled over a flat-iron doorstop in the hallway.

The little jade monkey gave me a permanently enchanting symbol for Mr. Van Hoek—at least for the remoteness and unreality about him. I remember seeing him briefly on several other occasions. Once he gave me a police whistle that I prized greatly. I think I felt, however, that he should have given me the monkey. The fact that he did not do so served to convince me that our relationship would never be very close. As a matter of fact, he did not fraternize with any of my family. He treated my father and mother—as he treated me—with great deference but with marked formality.

His influence on Aunt Tessie was not immediately apparent. But if she did not change at once, our attitude toward her did. The transformation was a subtle one— the kind that comes with discovering in somebody an unexpected talent that might be of profit to oneself. We immediately became more tolerant of Aunt Tessie. Our tensions relaxed, and we stopped torturing ourselves with the realization that we had an octopus under our roof. Our hopes in the matter we assuredly must have held in hair-spring balance. We never discussed Mr. Van Hoek. We never questioned Aunt Tessie about him at the table. From any realistic point of view, the thought that Aunt Tessie should actually have Mr. Van Hoek as a beau was still quite unacceptable.

Then one day the ultimate in the absurd happened. Aunt Tessie eloped with Mr. Van Hoek. Never, I am sure, was anything so infuriatingly unnecessary. Had we not been afraid of breaking the charm, we would have enthusiastically aided and abetted all along. We would certainly have done something sedate and nice for her at the church for a wedding. My father would have given her away, and I could have walked down the aisle—as I had once seen one of my playmates doing at his big sister's wedding—carrying the ring on a white silk pillow. And we could have had a splendid party afterward with all the punch that anybody could drink and all the cheese biscuits and chicken salad sandwiches and wedding cake that anybody could wish to stuff himself with. The joint celebration of Aunt Tessie's triumph and our release could have made us the talk of the town.

This was my line of thought, not necessarily my mother's. She had no patience with high-flown imagination or delusions of grandeur, but she had firm faith in decorum and propriety. And her sensibilities in these directions were now so brutally violated that she entirely forgot to be glad that Aunt Tessie was no longer under foot in our house.

"To think that your sister made this her home for over a year," said my mother, avoiding Aunt Tessie's name as if it now involved a taboo,"—to think that she made this her home for over a year and then ran over to Stanton to get married without letting us know. And in that ridiculous automobile! Of course, she was married by a justice of the peace. And she had the gall to go to Clarina's and ask her to call us by long distance telephone and give us the news."

Plainly Aunt Tessie had left us flat. We may have deserved exactly what we got; but at the time we could not afford to make any such admission. We were inclined to feel that the one thing right that Aunt Tessie had ever done in the world she had done in quite the wrong way. My mother, Aunt Allie, and all the other members of the family seemed to gloat—though perversely—in agreement on that point.

In the next six years Aunt Tessie lived in a great many places that seemed very far away and unusual to us: places like Parkersburg, West Virginia; Peoria, Illinois; Sioux City, Iowa; and Cincinnati, Ohio. We assumed that people used sewing machines in all these distant places.

"Your sister is certainly seeing the world," my mother occasionally remarked to my father. "A lot more than I've ever had a chance to see." (Real virtue, she implied, is seldom rewarded.)

In time, of course, we all came to luxuriate in Aunt Tessie's marital triumph and in her remoteness. As it turned out, she had by no means cut herself off from her family completely. She made one or two visits home without apologies for any previous slights. So far as we could see she was in many respects the same old Aunt Tessie, talking a great deal (and often incoherently), minding everybody's business except her own. Marriage had worked no marvelous sea-change, though it had given her a new topic of conversation and a new axis of reference:—"Van," whose praises she sang and whose opinions she cited on any and all occasions instead of quoting herself, as her old habit was. Indeed, she was almost as eccentric as she had ever been. But none of her eccentricities seemed to bother us any more—largely, I suppose, because we no longer had to accept responsibility for them. She even sounded moderately respectable when the *Advocate* reported:

"Mrs. Frederick Van Hoek's return to Bayesville for a brief visit is welcomed by a wide circle of relatives and friends." This statement was not true, but it looked good in print.

Mr. Van Hoek himself stayed in Peoria or Sioux City or wherever he happened to be, not bothering to put in another appearance. But Aunt Allie, who actually got up the nerve to go out for a visit, reported that he was "such a gentleman in his own house" and that the Van Hoeks usually "ate out." This settled at least the domestic question concerning the household; and for a time all else mysterious about the match seemed to dissolve.

Then, after years that still seem long to me, came the little yellow piece of paper—always bearing black news—from the telegraph office in the railway station: "Mr. Van Hoek passed away suddenly. Will bring body home Thursday. Tessie."

My father received the message at his office in the early afternoon. That night there was a solemn family conclave in our parlor. Aunt Allie was there, of course, and Cousin William had driven Aunt Clarina over from Stanton, picking up Uncle Alex on the way. My father and mother completed the inner council. The telegram lay unfolded on the console table in our hall as mute evidence, to the stream of lesser relatives and neighbors, that tragedy had befallen. Though the constant movement of people precluded any formality for the council, there could be no doubt about the unity of feeling.

"It's a damn—pardon, Aunt Emma—a great shame that the old gentleman couldn't have outlived Tessie," said Cousin William. "A darned shame that he had to up and die like this."

"She'll be awful at the funeral," said Aunt Allie, practically wringing her hands. "You know how Tessie acts. Why, she always made herself a sight crying at funerals of people she didn't even know. She'll just be hysterical, fit to be tied, and a disgrace to us all. We'll never have a proper funeral."

"Somebody else must have written the telegram," said Uncle Alexander. "It's worded far too sensible to be Tessie's."

"Does anybody have a black dress that she can wear and a black hat?" said Aunt Clarina. "I wouldn't be at all surprised if she turned up in something red or green. She never knew how to dress for anything, Tessie didn't. I declare I'd like her at least to look decent at the funeral."

People kept coming in saying, "Isn't it awful? Poor Miss Tessie!" And the family echoed "Awful, awful" with a kind of angry meaning all their own until the words became purely mechanical—that is, all the family except my mother who had a turkey in the stove and who took sufficient time off to baste it. She was facing the situation tight-lipped and was reserving her opinion about how Aunt Tessie might act and how Mr. Van Hoek's ungentlemanly defection might affect our future. Regardless of what else might happen, at least the funeral baked meats would be in order.

But if my mother preserved her outward calm, it was not because she hoped for the best. It existed rather in the face of a fully anticipated crisis soon to come. Plainly all the family intended to work themselves up to a state worthy of the prospect of having the old problem of Aunt Tessie to contend with all over again.

The minute I saw Aunt Tessie get off the train I ought to have guessed that she had tricked us once more. Though she was in no sense well dressed, she wore as sober black as even my mother could have prescribed. Without her usual make-up, she had a brownish pallor and her face was wrinkled like an over-baked apple; but she was remarkably composed.

During the next two days she shed some decorous tears at the most proper moments. But she never once gave in to weeping. We always expected her to, of course. We kept ourselves taut waiting for the moment when the floodgates would go down. But it never came.

I was left alone with her only once in our darkened parlor. Because I was now a gangling lad of twelve, I suppose, she did not reach out for me as she used to do. She did not make any of her old clumsy efforts to show me affection. She merely said with a soft huskiness, "You've grown up to be a great big boy, little Paulie. A great big boy. Your Uncle Van always said you were a fine boy. Yes, your Uncle Van always said that."

I was filled with pity for her, and even with a kind of affection. But my impulses to action were mixed. One impulse was to run to her and hug her as tightly as I could. Another was to get out of the house as quickly as possible.—I ended by making no move at all. Like my family, I still did not know what to do about Aunt Tessie.

But we did not have long to wait. After the funeral, the denouement came so simply that it was shocking. We were all back in the parlor again in the evening and a lull had come in the conversation.

"We must think of your future, Tessie," my father finally mustered the courage to say. "Perhaps we'd better make some plans."

There was an awesome silence. The reassumption of an old responsibility carried with it sufficient gravity.

"I've got a return ticket," said Aunt Tessie quietly, breaking the silence. "I'm leaving tomorrow. Going back to Cincinnati. That's what Van would want me to do."

"Oh, Tessie, you can't," said Aunt Allie, suddenly bursting into the sub-hysteria of which she had lately become capable. "You can't go back so soon. There's nobody in Cincinnati waiting for you. Why, we want you to stay here. Your home is here. Your loved ones are here. You can't go back to a strange city all by yourself. You can't. I won't stand for it."

"I'm going," said Tessie. "That's what Van would want me to do."

Then everybody began talking at once in high pitched voices, arguing with Aunt Tessie that she should stay. There had never been such bedlam—such loud blending of magnanimity and outrage. My mother assured Aunt Tessie that the spare room was still hers. Aunt Allie said she would "never speak" to Aunt Tessie again if she left, and offered to share her "light-housekeeping apartment." Aunt Clarina talked about the thought of Aunt Tessie's going back as a "disgrace" and insisted upon taking her back to Stanton; and Uncle Alexander thought that some arrangement could be made to make her happy in Treadwell, even though it was a "simple hamlet" and not a "great metropolis" like Cincinnati.

But Aunt Tessie seemed not to be listening to any of them. She just stared ahead of her, her gaunt old hands folded with serenity in her lap.

"That's what Van would want me to do," she persisted quietly. "I'm going back like I said."

The crescendo of alarm and indignation that mounted around her was completely ineffectual. Aunt Tessie sat like a rock. Nothing would move her. If she had achieved respectability as a widow that she'd never had otherwise, by all that was high and holy she was going to keep it for herself. That much ought to have been obvious to everybody present.

So the family had nothing to do finally but to withdraw in defeat.

The next afternoon we took Aunt Tessie down to the four o'clock train. How it happened I do not know, but it seemed that half the town turned out to see her off. Literally, everybody was there. The little platform of the buttercup yellow station was alive with the chatter of female voices. It was as if Aunt Tessie had actually become a celebrity by her cruel rejection of what we had so generously tried to offer.

"Tessie, Tessie," Aunt Allie sobbed to my mother when the train pulled out. "Nobody could ever drum any real sense into Tessie. She was always such a fool, such a fool!"

As for me, however, I was by no means so sure. Quite plainly Aunt Tessie had won again. Perhaps she shouldn't have, but she had. And that was all there was to it. Whatever guilt there might be was ours to expiate.

V

UNWILLINGLY TO SCHOOL

F my birth date, June 12, 1906, was something less than important as an eventful day for the world at large, my second landmark date, the day of my entrance into grammar school on September 2, 1912, was equally undistinguished. Yet just as the first date had been preceded by the San Francisco earthquake and fire on April 18-19, 1906, the second had been preceded by the sinking of the *Titanic* on April 14, 1912. This tragic event had unlike the San Francisco one become a definite part of my consciousness; for, though I was barely able to spell out a few words in the newspaper accounts at the time, I could look at the news photographs, the drawings, the cartoons, and could thus absorb some of the drama and the horror. In the following year a door-to-door book salesman supplied us with a picture book of the disaster that made the event even more vivid.

Certainly the national events of September 2 were hardly of such moment as to command the slightest attention of mine. For example, Colonel Roosevelt, who had been succeeded in the presidency by Taft, was being accused by Senator Boies Penrose of Pennsylvania and John D. Archibald, a vice-president of Standard Oil, of accepting funds from the large oil companies for his 1904 campaign and even of putting the squeeze on J. Pierpont Morgan for funds in addition to what this tycoon had already put up for the campaign. Cuban-American relations had been ruffled by an attack made by the Cuban Ambassador to Washington on the American Chargé in Havana, though President Taft was calmly playing golf in Beverly, Massachusetts, and was apparently contemplating nothing more serious in the immediate future than attending a horse show in Hamilton, Long Island.

A little later when I collected baseball cards from cigarette packages of my elders, I might have been interested in the fact that the Boston Americans had cinched the American League pennant and that there was uncertainty as to whether the Giants would wind up first in the National League. If I could have read it, I should have appreciated better a story about how a giant python was charmed by a whistled tune ("Music hath charms . . .") and a bottle of milk into releasing Charlie Snyder, a keeper in the Bronx Zoo, from a fatal embrace.

I mention the state of American letters at this point only because I was about to begin, with my learning to read, a period of literary consciousness. Though Dreiser had given the twentieth century a good literary start with *Sister Carrie* in 1900, there had not been many commanding figures who had not, like Henry James, carried over from the nineteenth. Certainly the summer reading successes of 1912 did not indicate much writing of unusually high or enduring quality. I have only to mention Mme. Elinor Glynn's *Halcyone* or W. B. Maxwell's *The Cotton Wool*. The same thing could be said about what was new on the autumn list: Sir Rider Haggard's *Marie*, May Sinclair's *The Flaw in the Crystal*, Anthony Partridge's thriller about the Anglo-French underworld, *The Count of St. Simon*. The British, not the Americans, were doing such writing as there was. In perspective the most interesting (and not for literary reasons) title on Appleton's fall list was *The Black Pearl*, described in the advertisement as "a passionate romance of the Arizona desert and the Rocky Mountains" written by the wife of the president of Princeton University, the first Mrs. Woodrow Wilson—an American this time, of course, and an unlikely one.

The drama was not much better, though in the New York theater, George Arliss was in the midst of his American success in *Disraeli*, John Drew was playing in *The Perplexed Husband*, Hale Hamilton was in *The N'er Do Well*, and William Farnum was starring in *The Littlest Rebel. The Pink Lady*, with its charming tunes, was in its last two weeks at the Amsterdam; and Reginald de Koven's popular *Robin Hood* was at the Knickerbocker.

As for me, I was walking the three quarters of a mile from my house to school, holding on to the hand of a pretty neighbor who was a junior or senior in the high-school division. The old building of the Bayesville Institute, as it was called, had been only a few blocks from our house. It had been a large frame structure designed in an approximation of the Victorian Gothic. Painted light gray, it had the inevitable green blinds and green trim of our region, and a stately bell tower. This last I had watched fall down the year before in a great upsurge of flames and smoke and with a last mournful clang of the bell—like the death, I imagined, of a fire-dragon. All the neighborhood children except me reacted in the normal way: that is, with joy at the sight of a burning school house and at the prospect of an unexpected vacation. I found no pleasure in the experience. The new building of the Bayesville Grammar and High School was a massive pile of bright red brick designed to be fireproof. It had no bell tower; but there was an imposing portico with gleaming white columns. Victorian Gothic, or an attempt in that direction, had been succeeded by the Classic Revival, symbolizing a new era in education that I was unwittingly helping to initiate.

Being totally innocent of nursery schools and kindergartens (none had been available to me), I was entering my first school of any kind. Yet my mother had no notion of marching up to school as other parents did, with me in tow. That procedure was undignified and unnecessary. Besides, other children would be going from the neighborhood, and I might as well learn independence from the start. There was a concession, nevertheless, when Edith Collins graciously offered to serve as my mother's surrogate. For my part, since I fell easily in love with pretty young women, I thought the idea splendid.

I had less enthusiasm and assurance, on the other hand, when my guide released her firm grip at the door of the first-grade classroom and I suddenly found myself adrift in a crowd of children who all seemed to be total strangers. When I was firmly but not ungently thrust into a desk by a tall, thin, goggle-eyed teacher named Miss Naylor, I was all but paralyzed by panic and homesickness. The two hours in the morning that I stayed in the room seemed about as long as any period of time I had ever endured. In the end and at long last somebody took me home, where I clutched my mother's skirt and dissolved into tears. A fine start toward independence this was!

Education always begins hard. But I assumed it was necessary; so I resolved to stick it out—at least for a year, by which time I might figure out some other solution. The second year, however, proved better. After skipping something called the advanced first grade, I found myself with some of the slightly older children whom I had known well: for example, my peppery little redheaded neighbor named Fred Collins; a handsome, bright, and warm lad called John Morrell; Elise Wesson, my blonde and sprightly second cousin; and the prettiest curly-headed and black-eyed little brunette I ever saw or could imagine, Elizabeth Marlin. Elizabeth was the object of my first romance. I still remember the thrill that I got when she slyly slipped a note to me in class or saved a piece of cake for me from her lunch box. And there was even a greater thrill when our teacher took us for "nature walks" and little picnics in wooded areas nearby, and I walked along holding her hand. I dreamed about her at night; and on one occasion I solemnly announced to my parents my plan to marry her—and that in the near future. I had worked out all the details of where we could live: the attic could easily be made comfortable, and there were "houses" in the magnolia trees. Neither parent offered any strong objection. An end was put to this eventuality by nothing less than the fact that Elizabeth's family moved to Texas. I never heard from her again, but I never forgot her.

What I did in school seemed less important than the people with whom I did those things: I mean reading and writing, and sums in arithmetic, and the apples and boxes that we drew in the "art" period, and the songs that we learned from "Good morning to you, Good morning to you, Good morning, dear teacher, and how do you do?" to *"Sur le pont d'Avignon, on y danse."*

Fred Collins was my rough-and-tumble no-romantic-nonsense kind of friend. With him I climbed trees, shot air rifles, built forts in his garden, rode bicycles, hopped tail-gates of farm wagons, played mumblety peg in the cool earth underneath his house, and wrestled on a sand pile in his backyard. Though he was usually warm and generous, sometimes his anger flared up; and at the end of the day I sometimes went home with his threat echoing in my ears: "I'm gonna beat you up tomorrow!" This I knew very well he could do if he took half a notion to, for I was not a good fighter and he always outwrestled me. But I also knew that he was blessed with a short memory and that after a night's sleep he would completely forget the threats of the previous day.

All in all, I had a good deal of admiration and affection for Fred. But John Morrell was the friend to whom I felt closest and whom I treasured most. He came from a family of extraordinary charm and intelligence. His mother I regarded as a dazzling beauty possessed of a softness and sweetness of manner that I could not imagine it possible to find in anyone else. If I had found it necessary to choose a substitute for my own mother, I should not have hesitated to choose her. (In fact, I acquired a certain amount of comfort in the thought that I had her, as it were, in reserve!) If I had looked at John's father with a critical eye, I might have found him ungainly, for he was tall and gangling and his thick glasses made his eyes look abnormally large. But I did not view him in that way, and I could find no fault with a father who was always interested in a creative way in what we were doing, who played games with us, read to us, and took us to matinées at the moving picture theater.

He had gone to school at The Citadel and even as a young man had been elected to the state legislature and had been appointed a colonel on the governor's staff. (His silver sword hung on the living-room wall.) Thus he was called Colonel Morrell. What happened to his political career I do not know. I do remember that his views were often unorthodox. For example, when he was editor of the *Advocate* he supported a politician named Cole L. Blease, anathema to the "best" people who regarded Blease as a rabble-rouser fit only for the "wool-hat boys" and the "lint heads." Since John stoutly maintained his father's views, I had many a hot argument with him—without knowing more than what I had caught from snatches of conversation of my elders. I also argued with him, as little boys argue, about the War Between the States. John attributed to it none of the romance and glamor that I felt. If he had repeated his father accurately (and he did not quite do so), he would have said that the Confederates were the biggest damn fools in history. To me even such a thought, much less a statement, was sacrilegious. (*Nefas nefandum,* as Virgil and long-toothed little Miss Villard taught us to say some years later in the high-school Latin class.) Yet these arguments never really came between John and me and never made me cease loving his father.

In time something happened that I did not understand, and the family plainly had to live in reduced circumstances—though never with a lack of grace or with any indication of a need for pity. Then one day a most horrible thing occurred: Colonel Morrell was killed as he fell under the wheels of a passenger train that he was trying to catch as it was leaving our station. Nothing short of the death of my father could have affected me more.

All through my grammar school days John was, in spite of our differences of opinion, not only my friend but also my defender. Like Fred, he was sturdier than I. Knowing as much and recognizing that bullies among our contemporaries had little trouble spotting my weakness, he early made it clear to me and to our world at large that he was determined to defend me whenever I needed him. I would, of course, have done the same for him to the best of my ability. But he was quite able to take care of himself; and while on a number of occasions he intervened effectively for me, I never had an occasion to return the compliment.

Elise Wesson was my cousin and sister-substitute. She, John, and I formed an all but inseparable trio. Blonde, pretty, and pert, and with a whimsical turn of mind, Elise nevertheless from her earliest childhood had a touch of the imperious that enabled her to get her way not only with me but also with everybody else for that matter—when she chose. She lived in the finest house in town (a little estate in itself) and she had everything she could desire. Her mother dressed her out of the "Lilliputian Bazaar" catalogue of Best & Company with things sent down periodically "on approval" from New York. She had every toy and childhood gadget available. She had the best of tricycles and bicycles to ride, and later horses, and still later automobiles—I mean Buicks and Cadillacs, not Fords, Maxwells, or Essexes—or nothing, like some of the rest of us.

But at this point the most important circumstance was that she was mistress of a playhouse the likes of which no other child in town could approach. Among other things, it had a complete kitchen with running water and a stove that burned wood like the big ones. All summer long for several years, John and I were official "boarders," and we were expected to be on hand for midday dinner on whatever days we were summoned. What Elise did not prepare herself on her remarkably efficient little stove, dignified Mary Wayne, wearing her white apron and cap, brought down from the kitchen in the big house on a covered tray.

With all her competence and basic intelligence, Elise either was no student or did not choose to be one. And help with her lessons was the compensation she expected or exacted from me for "board," transportation to and from school which her family frequently provided, and numerous other favors that I received. But let me back up a bit. "Help" is a vast understatement. I was supposed to do her lessons for her—write the sentences, do the sums, draw the maps, or whatever was supposed to be done. All this unethical service (though it hardly occurred to either of that it was unethical) I performed as unquestioned routine, and I continued to do so through grammar and high school. Even when she was in college in Boston years later, she would send special delivery letters to me saying "I need a paper on 'The Clowns in Shakespeare' (or 'The Congress of Vienna' or 'The Diet of Tree Frogs'). Please send it to me at once." Sometimes I rebelled and said, "Go jump into the Charles River or the lake that I think is in the Common." But at other times I put down my work and wrote the paper. I would have been properly horrified if I had caught one of my own fellow college students submitting a paper that he had plagiarized or had had somebody else to write. (I maintained a Puritan conscience.) But somehow Elise was above wrongdoing, and I never had one twinge of remorse for the service that I performed for her.

So much for some of the most important of my school friends who, I think it is fair to say, educated me while I educated them. My teachers must have taught me something, too, though it is strange how little of them I can remember and, therefore, how limited their influence must have been. Miss Naylor was chiefly kind and painstaking in a gaunt way. Mrs. Younger was far jollier and more inventive. She let some of us come to her house on Saturday morning to sit on the floor in her big front hall or, in the spring, on the porch shaded by camellia trees full of red blossoms, where we drew and colored or made presents for our parents out of multicolored sheets of blotting paper, sandpaper, and felt: useless pen wipers or book marks or surfaces for striking matches and so on. Then there was tiny Miss Wardman with brown eyes and turned-up nose, whom we all loved merely because she was pretty. Again, there was poor Miss Phelps, with a kind of grayish mashed-in face and colorless hair, who hilariously mispronounced words that most of us knew how to pronounce. I

John Stuart Mill began the study of Greek at three. At five Mozart appeared in concert. At six Thomas Babington Macaulay was at work on a compendium of world history. Fortunately, my mother had not read *Tristram Shandy* and she thus could not have known the way in which a discussion of precocity ended in that fascinating work: "But you forget the great Lipsius, quoth Yorick, who composed a work the day he was born;—They should have wiped it up, said my uncle Toby, and said no more about it." Yet perhaps the best comment of all on my performance has been made by the contemporary playwright, Edward Albee, who said, "I wrote poetry when I was six, which was before the age of reason." Indeed!

However auspicious or inauspicious my beginning in a career as writer might have been, my literary interest had to be shared with another enthusiasm—music. For a long time I had been supplied with toy musical instruments—pianos, violins, horns, and so on. In fact, I had an unusually large toy piano at which I gave noise concerts full of tone clusters and atonality—in a style, though I did not know it, far in advance of my time. My father, who had no ear for music at all, was so impressed that he decided I should have music lessons at once; or, maybe, on the other hand he thought that some formal training might lessen the noise in the house. At any rate, he promptly bought an upright Harvard piano for me, moved it into the parlor, and enrolled me in the music class of Miss Laney Collins who lived just a few doors down the street. This arrangement did serve to lessen the banging, for it involved me in such things as scales, five-finger exercises, and little pieces that I had to work out laboriously. (One of these latter called "Playing in the Field" caused some questioning on the part of my father when it turned up sans quotation marks on Miss Laney's monthly bill.)

Every child is a genius before he is ten, and almost none is after that. To the theory that my father must have been fooled by the illusion of some trace of genius in me I attribute the fact that he not only replaced my toy piano with a full-sized one but he also bought me a standard Remington typewriter. He seemed to be hedging his bets. If I didn't make the grade in music, I might do it in journalism or literature. So at a comparatively early stage, I was encouraged to let two arts join hands.

Since at the time, radio was some years off, television was even further, and phonographs were just beginning their real development, I had few opportunities to hear a wide variety of recorded music. The time was not far away from the little old Edison machines with their curious cylindrical discs, which had been replaced by platters played on machines with wheezy morning-glory horns. My chief means of hearing good music fairly professionally produced was, therefore, in the Lyceum programs given in the school auditorium four or five evenings in the winter and in Chautauqua programs given in tents in the summer. Another source came through a curious friendship that I developed with a talented blind woman named Miss Vann Hunter, who had had a good deal of musical training in a college for the sightless. Her huge old house had a parlor dominated by a Chickering square piano of elaborately carved teakwood, at which she would from time to time sit and sing arias from operas with me as her sole audience. Frequently, I listened in a state of near trance, a condition induced not only by the music but also by the cool red-carpeted room darkened by heavy draperies and smelling delicately of furniture polish and dried rose petals.

At the time I thought I had seen nothing more impressive than Miss Vann as she sat at the piano with her white marble arms and her classic profile under dark hair severely drawn back into a knot at the nape of her neck, letting her big voice roll forth with all the effortlessness in the world.

It is true that when she sang as soloist in church cantatas and oratorios, she made movements with her lips that caused her to look grotesque. But when she was looking away from me, as she did when she sang in her parlor, I could imagine that she was Mmes. Alda, Schumann-Heink, Homer, and Matzenauer all rolled into one. So when I was about eight or nine, I conceived the scheme of writing an opera for her. I got only so far as a sketchy libretto and one aria, which I demonstrated by playing on the piano and singing (both very badly). The only thing that I remember about the libretto was that it was violent and romantic, roughly in the manner of Lorenzo da Ponte. (Miss Vann had told me the stories of the most famous operas, slightly bowdlerized, and had given me a little book about opera written for children. Thus I had something to plagiarize.) As poetry, the aria was hardly better than my first effort, though it had a word or two that made it either slightly more sophisticated—or trite, as one wishes to judge. Fortunately, I remember only the opening lines—

> Thou'rt as fair as the rose
> That wafts its sweet perfume
> On the evening breeze,
> On the evening breeze.

(I'm afraid that "perfume" came out in the music as "per-fyu-um," though "evening" was gracefully and properly reduced to two syllables.)

So, after a fashion, in this ill-conceived and executed attempt, literature and music did strive to merge. I must admit that I often found it easier to devote my time to the typewriter than to the piano, for exercises and studies by Czerny and Two-Part Inventions of Bach at times became colossal bores; and I had to be forced into pursuit of them by my mother, who might not have acted so much in the interest of music as in that of protecting my father's investment in my study of it.

The sounds that I was ultimately able to get out of the piano sometimes surprised and delighted me, but there was always somebody—usually a pert little girl— who could play better than I and by so doing put me to shame. There were other causes of shame also. My male peers, however well they may have started, usually stuck to their lessons for only a month or two. They, therefore, were inclined to regard piano playing as sissy. Then there were recitals—those devilish devices that caused me to lose sleep for nights before that horrible moment when I had to march all alone across a stage, sit down at a piano, and force my nervous, jerking fingers to produce an inane collection of sounds to be thrust into a sea of hostile faces and ears to the side and in front of me.

For a time at this point I decided that a literary career was easier to pursue than a musical one. The reasoning was simple. While I was at my typewriter, I was not sequestered in a parlor with musical notes in front of me that somebody else had written and with exercises to do so that my fingers would be limber. In my little nook in the back hall I was on my own, and my limits were only the limits of my imagination. My typing system I worked out for myself—to my later regret, I might add. It was the well-known but ill-advised two-finger hunt-and-peck method. When I got to high school, I tried to learn the touch system; but my reflexes were all programmed, and it was too late.

But with even the most elementary method, practice can bring speed; and I plugged away joyfully at it, turning out verses, stories, little neighborhood newspapers, plays for puppets and for people (small ones).

On the side. as soon as I could manage a canvas bag

with Saturday Evening Post stamped on it, I set out peddling that magazine, to which I soon added *The Literary Digest*. How much I read in the copies of both that I did not sell, I do not remember exactly. I also went through some other family magazines on the pulp side, not so much for the reading matter in them as for the puzzles and the accompanying ads that offered a rich reward for anybody who solved them. The most common puzzle was the one that had a number of faces hidden in a pen-and-ink drawing of a landscape. The ad of the puzzle that I recall most ruefully promised nothing less than a Shetland pony. Since the father of one of my playmates had once given him a pony with a little wicker cart to go with it, I became obsessed with the idea of having one of these elegant pets myself. (I never envied my friends who had goats and little wagons. Goats smelled bad and would butt you down on the slightest provocation or none at all.) So I found all the faces in the puzzle and sent in my solution, carefully drawn so that there could be no mistaking about my having won. Back in the mail about a week later came a congratulatory letter advising me that I had accumulated twenty-five thousand votes in the pony contest and that I could earn more of the necessary points by selling some very popular postcards with floral and scenic designs, a package of which was already on the way. Not willing to lose such a splendid advantage in the contest as I already had, I canvassed the neighborhood, often eliciting irate remarks from females who had been interrupted in the midst of their afternoon naps or called away from cake batter. But after I sold the first batch of cards and was credited with several thousand additional points, more points were still needed. The race was neck and neck. Another batch of cards was sold with the same results. So on and on until I gave up in disgust without ever seeing even a picture of a pony. In order to get something else in a different kind of contest, I later sold blueing. That, too, was a fizzle.

As for children's magazines, Elise Wesson, (always with the best) took the *St. Nicholas Magazine,* which she let me see from time to time. John Morrell and I preferred *The American Boy.* And I finally found a less slick publication called *The Boy's Magazine,* which appealed to me chiefly because it had a generous policy of publishing contributions by subscribers. Since "Grandfather's Clock," my bibliography had been at a standstill; and I needed badly to be in print again. So I scratched my head and cranked up my typewriter. In a year or two the magazine had published a number of my things: two or three stories, a how-to-do-it piece, and even several cartoons. (I had sent off a quarter for an introductory lesson in how to draw and had set out to teach myself.)

One of the published stories (*horresco referens,* I shudder to refer to it) was called "Mapsuot's Leap." Mapsuot was an Indian chieftain; and, as everyone should have known, there were an awful lot of Indians, chieftains and beautiful princesses, who jumped off rocks for one reason or another—but chiefly because they loved somebody who did not love back. Like a New England lady poet whom I have previously quoted, I had never seen a mountain and I had never seen a moor, whatever the latter was; but somewhere I had acquired the notion that practically every high rock anywhere had had some noble-blooded Indian leap off it. All other notions about Indians, maybe including that one, I had got from Westerns at the movies and the magazines that I read, not to mention the Indian games that we all played. So Mapsuot in full regalia and warpaint, his full-feathered headdress fluttering in the breeze, leaped to his death, and all for love. Fortunately, the waters of memory have obliterated the other stories, which could only have been worse.

The how-to-do-it piece was more workmanlike and thus more admirable. Into the neighborhood had come a new boy named Henry Greenfield, who, finding us in need of advancing from the age of tin-can telephones strung on wrapping twine, initiated me into some of the secrets of electricity and suggested that we build a telegraph set. By this time I had acquired a Chemcraft set and had set up a "laboratory" in a corner of the barn because my mother would not allow it in the house. I had turned red liquid into white liquid and vice versa and I had mixed powders in a test tube which I had held over a candle to produce nothing more notable than a fine stink. But beyond playing with a flashlight, I had never done anything involving electricity. The thing to do, Henry said, was to go down to the Central Office (the little telephone exchange), back of which was a lot of discarded electrical materials: wire, magnets, old dry-cell batteries. Out of some of this stuff we got a little apparatus, that, powered by a dozen or more old batteries properly connected, gave off a click similar to the sound made by the telegraph keys in the railroad station. Henry was the inventive genius and the electrical engineer. I was the reporter, and I did an article, with a pen and ink drawing, to show exactly how any intelligent boy could do what Henry and I did at absolutely no cost—or almost none. When this article appeared, my reputation soared among my peers who had shrugged off my melodramatic attempts at fiction.

If I wanted to write, I had to read. This conclusion I had reached at a precociously early date; and I had been reading everything that came into sight and within reach almost from the day I could make words out of collections of letters. My reading was all along without guidance and almost without discrimination. Not once at any stage did my parents exert any censorship or suggest any interdiction. The usual books—fairy tales, Bible stories, tales from Shakespeare and Dickens—I read because people gave them to me on birthdays and at Christmas. A particularly fascinating piece of literature that I got hold of was an illustrated children's version of the first two books of *Gulliver's Travels,* which Fred Collins and I read at the same time. Any suggestion of Swift's satire was, of course, completely lost on us. But the idea of the little people so convincingly described gave us days of fantasizing in the area bordering a creek in the pasture back of his house, where we discussed what we would do as co-Gullivers if several boat loads of Lilliputians should by some chance come sailing up the stream. We were not very much interested in being Gullivers among the Brobdingnagians. I had already encountered the Giant of Doubting Castle in *Pilgrim's Progress,* which my father had read to me, and various other giants like the one in *Jack and the Bean-Stalk;* thus I would not have willingly chosen that kind of experience.

On quite a different level there was another book that made a great impression on me. Read to me by Aunt Allie before I was quite able to manage it on my own, Anna Sewell's *Black Beauty* became an early favorite. This autobiography of a horse told with remarkable suspense and little sentimentality I thought could hold its own against any other kind of story. Of course, with my phobia being what it was, I trembled through the chapter of the fire, the result of a careless hostler's letting Dick Towler get into the stable with a pipe in his mouth. And I can still feel the pathos of Beauty's later years when I encounter the illustration in the small 1894 edition of the book with two cabman's horses, heads lowered, standing in plainly inclement weather, over the caption: "Sometimes driver and horse have to wait for hours in the rain or frost."—I am afraid that Aunt Allie also read to me such dubious classics as *Miss Minerva and William Greenhill* and *Mrs. Wiggs of the Cabbage Patch,* but these I have all but totally forgotten.

On rainy afternoons and holidays all through grammar school I was likely to be found going through the *Book of Knowledge,* reading the volumes as one does an encyclopedia, or doing the same thing with an old edition of *Stoddard's Lectures.* Through these latter I traveled over Europe, accumulating all kinds of odd information about odd places—like, for example, the fact that *Dam Bad Rum* was not a profane comment on an alcoholic beverage but a sign in a Swedish hotel to indicate the ladies' bathroom.

During the Christmas season there were always some books for sale in my father's store: illustrated linen and paper ones for the little children and others for the older. Of the latter I contrived to read as many as possible before somebody bought them. In so doing I became an authority on such classics as Horatio Alger's *Phil the Fiddler, Paul the Peddler,* and *Sink or Swim;* and I learned well their lessons of how to succeed in a capitalist world by really trying. I also got hold of some Tom Swift books, my earliest introduction to respectable science fiction.

My warm interest in the Confederacy led me to read all the volumes in the "Little Colonel" series. Since the little colonel was a girl, I concealed the fact that I was reading the series from my male friends, discussing the books only with Elise. (She, incidentally, tried to get me to read the books about the "Five Little Peppers," but I refused, having not the slightest interest in "how they grew.") One of my other favorite books was Thomas Nelson Page's *The Two Little Confederates,* the adventures of whose joint heroes in helping the Southern troops round up some Yankee marauders were most moving. After the beginning of World War I, I changed my allegiance partly because of the "Boy Allies" books, each new volume of which I awaited with genuine suspense.

I haunted the public library: that is, when it was hauntable. It was housed in a ridiculous and tiny one-story structure, almost a perfect square and otherwise featureless, that had been used as an Episcopal chapel. When communicants became too few to make it practicable for a priest to come over from a neighboring parish, the diocese abandoned the mission and sold their uncanonical building to the town, which put it to its present use. Books were available only on two afternoons in the week and on Saturday mornings, and the attendants were usually a spinster who was the chairman of the library Committee of the sponsoring Civic League and a high-shcool senior who was paid a pittance for her highly inexpert service. I was on hand as much as possible—and particularly on the days on which new books were put out.

As a result I picked up books in mint condition and read them before anybody else in town had had the slightest chances to do so, whether they were "Penrod" novels by Booth Tarkington or much headier stuff. (The so-called librarians almost never cracked a book except to apply a rubber stamp to the back of the cover and to write in a number with indelible ink.) My grabbing whatever turned up on the "new" shelf contributed in a remarkable way to my enlightenment. On one occasion, for example, I walked away with a novel by Joseph Hergesheimer called *Cytherea*. Even at thirteen or fourteen I knew that I had acquired something quite unlike anything I had previously encountered in this lurid story in which the heroine, exhausted from a passionate illicit love affair, dies in the squalor and filth of a Cuban village hotel. This impression was strongly reinforced when I learned that the Baptist minister had checked the book out when I brought it back, had presumably read it, and then consigned it to the flames of his kitchen range. On the following Sunday I heard him preach a sulphurous sermon on the subject. It was one of the few that I listened to; and I did so with a feeling of smug superiority. He and I were the only people in town who knew all about "free love," and we were likely to be the only ones for some time to come. (Luckily, he had no idea that I had read the book, too)—I also later read Elinor Glynn's *Three Weeks* and from the lady's skillful asterisks got as much sex education as my understanding allowed. I should have aspired to higher things.

But I would do myself, and truth, an injustice if I gave the impression that I read chiefly such trash. By taking anything that came along, I also encountered history, biography, drama, and not a little respectable fiction. As I increased my reading skill I had fairly early reached out beyond the few books that we had in our house to the conveniently near library of my older cousin William, who bought books in sets: the *Harvard Classics*, the "complete" Mark Twain, the collected O. Henry, and so forth. I read straight through O. Henry, which was no great accomplishment. *Huckleberry Finn*, *Tom Sawyer*, its sequel, and *The Connecticut Yankee* all became favorites, though I could not make out *Joan of Arc* and some of the other Twain books. My assault on the *Harvard Classics* was not at this time signally successful. But I tried. Though I could not, of course, read such things as *The Wealth of Nations* and *The Origin of Species*, I turned the pages, and I at least got the notion that these were important books. I did read at a rather early age all of the two-volume edition of *Les Miserables* in the library of another friend, led to it by my interest in the story of the stolen candlesticks that I had found in a collection of stories for children.

If my reading in fiction was in the category of the catch-as-catch-can, the poetry that I was encouraged to read, or rather to memorize, in grammar school was unfortunately prescribed. And it was hardly calculated (as I look back on it now) to develop a superior taste for the form. In spite of our Southernness, we allowed the New England poets to continue to dominate our textbooks—for the simple reason that most of these were published in the North, particularly in Boston. Thus, from the first grade we chanted about autumn in Massachusetts rather than in South Carolina:

> The goldenrod is yellow,
> The corn is turning brown,
> The trees in apple orchards
> With fruit are bending down.

Paying little attention to what from our point of view were anachronisms, we even drew pictures of goldenrod and corn and overloaded apple trees—the last being easy because we had only to do fat blobs of green supported by short brown sticks and generously dotted with red. But when we got to "The Gentian's (so in my imagination) bluest fringes were curling in the sun," nobody would admit to ever seeing a Gentian. But we could agree with Gelett Burgess in regard to his purple cow that we had rather see than be one.

Next there was "The Psalm of Life"—inescapable, patriarchial, bearded H. W. Longfellow. And over and over before the class or at the Friday afternoon "speaking," somebody was called on to go through "Tell me not in mournful numbers." Since numbers still meant numerals to me, I amused myself for some time in wondering what the mournful numbers could be, and I went carefully at least through the numerals from one to ten without being able to decide: One—loneliness? Two—that's a pair, so certainly not! Three—a crowd and somebody left out?—It was no good! I also, I might add, went through the same difficulty with a line in a lugubrious song that we sang on a special occasion (of which more later): that is, "When we were numbered with the slain" from "Just before the Battle, Mother." For this, however, the solution was a bit easier because I conjured up a picture of some kind of medical corpsman wandering over the battle field painting numbers on the corpses with prepared chalk or iodine. The idea was ghoulish, I admitted, but it was a possibility.

There was also a battle poem that we were forced to memorize, this time by the English poet Robert Southey:

> On Linden when the sun was low,
> All bloodless lay th' untrodden snow,
> And dark as winter was the flow
> Of Isar rolling rapidly.

Then the drums started beating "in the dead of night"; and, as we recited the poem, the sing-song rhythm and the sinister suggestion were all that mattered. Nobody bothered to ask where or what Linden and the Isar were, or what the fighting was all about. Poetry was chiefly sound: it didn't have to mean anything. (Many years later didn't Archibald McLeish back us up in this conclusion when he said "A poem should not mean but be"? So "Hohenlinden" joined the ritual of pure incantation.

For quite a different purpose, we memorized still another war poem, typically tear-jerking—this time by a Georgia poet. It was called "Little Giffen of Tennessee by Francis Orray Ticknor" (sic)—we said the whole thing as if the author were a part of the title, and then began our recitation:

> Out of the focal and foremost fire,
> Out of the hospital walls as dire,
> Smitten of grape shot and gangrene,

> Eighteenth battle and he sixteen—
> Spectre such as you seldom see,
> Little Giffen of Tennessee.

The occasion was Memorial Day—Southern Memorial Day on May 10, not May 31. The observance was sponsored by the local chapter of the United Daughters of the Confederacy. My mother joined the organization because she was entitled to, but she hated going to the meetings and seldom attended. Nevertheless, early in the morning on May 10 she could be found on the back porch sewing magnolia leaves on a frame for me to take to school, wearing it with my head and one shoulder and arm through the hole of the wreath.

At the schoolhouse interested townspeople gathered with a good many ladies of the U.D.C. on hand in white dresses with ribbons displayed crosswise on their ample bosoms. There were also a few Confederate veterans, some bright-eyed and cocky in spite of their age and other crusty ones bent over canes. They appropriately wore their old uniforms, or parts of them; and somebody usually had a tattered regimental flag. A speech—intended to be impassioned but really dull and meaningless—was made by a local politician. We sang several patriotic songs like "Just before the Battle, Mother," "Maryland, My Maryland," and the one about the "bonnie blue flag";

> Hurrah! Hurrah! for Southern rights, Hurrah!
> Hurrah! Hurrah for the bonnie blue flag
> That bears a single star.

We waved flags during the singing, but they had many stars and bars on them. So I had difficulty figuring out why we were singing about a flag with only one star. But no matter. After the singing was over, we marched double-file, wreaths over heads and shoulders, down the one-mile stretch to the town cemetery. Here we disbanded to distribute our wreaths, draping them over the little crosses that the U.D.C. chapter had placed on the graves of departed veterans. I put my wreath on the grave of my paternal grandfather, who I later learned had really not gone to the war at all but had sent a "substitute"—an arrangement to allow a plantation owner, whose eligible sons had already gone to the army, to keep his farm going. There was good common sense in this circumstance, but absolutely no glamor.

Anyway, the grandfather (long dead before I was born) got decorated. We all assembled again at the cemetery well. Somebody blew taps, and we marched back double-file to school, by this time hot, sweaty, and disgruntled.

In one of the stories that I read from Cousin William's collection, O Henry said that to be a man one had to experience love, poverty, and war. Or that's what I think he said. If he did, I had made only a small start on my real "education"—and that in the main vicariously.

VI

MISS MALVINA: AN INTERLUDE

O NE week in the summer of 1918 I was allowed to write the "Citizen of the Week" story in the *Advocate;* and I decided that it should be about Miss Malvina Withers, the village librarian. I'd say that she was then in her late thirties; but she really did not look it. Her hair was still dark and glossy (I couldn't swear that Pearline didn't doctor it up a bit in her popular just-opened beauty "shoppe"), and she wore it with two large buns sticking out from both ears. The hair-do was designed to make her look very much in the current mode ("cootie garages," the soldiers called them), and the sweater and skirt combination was intended to make her look younger than she was. She wasn't bad looking, though no one would call her a beauty. Her thin features were delicate rather than pinched, and her eyes were pleasingly deep without being soulful. Maybe her neck would not stand too close inspection—but there was no reason for my going over her with a magnifying glass. She was of medium height, and her figure was pretty good, though her legs might have been a little thin for the taste of the boys who hung around Riddle's drugstore corner.

Miss Malvina was the daughter of Montague Withers, who had clerked so long at the New York

Racket Store that he looked, talked, and acted like old Mr. Goldstein, who owned it. He was a tall man with a droopy mustache. His wife was one of those wispy, retiring women who rarely went out of the house even to do shopping for clothes. She did all her housework, including her laundry.

There were three other children besides Malvina. An older sister was married to a scales salesman and lived in Dayton, Ohio. A younger brother was a clerk in a shoe store in Augusta. Still another brother died of typhoid fever at sixteen. That completed the vital statistics.

Maybe Miss Malvina was not the best looking member of the family, but she was the brightest and she got the best education. In high school she led her classes, being especially good in English, history, and music. When she graduated she wrote the class poem and the class song and delivered the valedictory. There was no doubt that she finally had the very center of the stage. Her father was as proud as Punch, and right there decided that she'd have the best education that he could mortgage himself to get for her. And, indeed, she did get it. She went to Chadwick, as fashionable and as good a college as any other in the state. She did well there, too.

I got interested in her when near my twelfth birthday I wheedled Colonel Morrell's successor, Mr. Peabody, into giving me a part-time job on the *Advocate* in order to get practical experience in journalism. I was allowed to write some of the "social notes" like "Mr. and Mrs. John Greene had dinner with their relatives in Trenton last Sunday," and "Mrs. James Perryman of Greenville is visiting her sister-in-law, Mrs. Percy Spears, on Oak Street this week," or "Mrs. Gerald Badham entertained her bridge club at her home on Plum Tree Lane on Thursday afternoon. A sweets course was served." I was also allowed to write some little human-interest stories. In order to do so, I had a wonderful time looking over old yellowed and foxed files of the paper.

I couldn't help noticing that the *Advocate* was forever carrying little items about Miss Malvina, about her winning an essay contest at Chadwick or being a junior marshal (whatever that is) or appearing in a recital. Colonel Morrell told me that the stories were written from notes scribbled on brown wrapping paper by Mr. Withers and passed along to the editor, lest otherwise he "might not have heard."—And when Miss Malvina came home for vacations, she was constantly appearing on programs of the Epworth League, the Woman's Club (as the old Civic League was later called), and the U.D.C., either singing solos or reading original poems or papers. People still remember the paper she read on "The Legacy of Stonewall Jackson," full of fine and stirring sentiment. She was called upon to give it on every possible occasion; and finally the *Advocate* printed the whole thing, "by popular request."

Without doubt, nobody showed more brilliant promise than Miss Malvina. People like Mrs. Augustus Preston, perennial president of the Woman's Club and Democratic Committeewoman for the state, were always saying Miss Malvina would make a name for herself that would "bring honor and renown to our fair little city."

As I figured it, it was hardly Miss Malvina's fault that she didn't. When she finished college, she got a good job in a big school like the Sheffield High School, and she was immediately asked to sing in the choir of the First Presbyterian Church and to be a soloist in the Sheffield Oratorio Society. Her picture was all over the papers. She was certainly on her way to something like the Metropolitan Opera Company, being able to outsing even a local celebrity like Miss Van Hunter.

Then in a second year a strange thing happened. She completely lost her voice, not only her singing voice but also her speaking voice. The circumstance was sufficiently tragic as you may well believe. All at once her promising career came to an end. She simply came home and shut herself in. For several years nobody saw her. Then her voice partially came back and she ventured out again, very shyly at first as if she had committed some sort of crime. But most of the time she spent behind the trellises of thick kudzu vine that surrounded the Withers' home, defeated and wraithlike.

It was Mrs. Preston who decided that Miss Malvina might still have a useful career. The idea involved the library, which Mrs. Preston had for several years determined to move out of the drab little building in which it was housed. She won her battle not only to the extent of getting an appropriation from the town council but also some other funds of undetermined origin. A regular librarian would now be needed, and Miss Malvina was the best qualified person in the whole area.

The library had been relocated on the second floor of the "City Hall," an old two-story building with sprawling romanesque arches framing glass windows on the first floor. It used to be a bank; and the second floor was used for offices, some for the bankers and some for professional people. The library occupied several of the old offices from which the partitions had been removed.

When Miss Malvina took charge, the basic collection consisted of an eleventh edition of the *Encyclopedia Britannica,* a set of *Stoddard's Lectures,* the *Library of Southern Literature* ("graciously presented by the Abijah Welsh Chapter of the United Daughters of the Confederacy in memory of the glorious conduct of Sergeant Welsh at Antietam"), the

Harvard Classics (donated by the Civic League from the "proceeds of a silver tea on October 17, 1917"), a set of *Sir Walter Scott* with bad print and yellowed paper, the "Little Colonel" series, a set called *Great Orations,* and a highly miscellaneous and badly organized assortment of several hundred volumes, old and new.

The job not only transformed Miss Malvina; she transformed the library. There was no dust on the books. Maps and pictures were on the walls, and the rental shelves were bright with jackets of the latest novels and biographies. Miss Malvina read *The New York Times* and the *Atlantic Monthly* religiously, and she really knew what was what in the world of books. In fact, she was as well read as somebody in New York itself.

Just as she was alert and up-to-date, she was no prude. Being weak-voiced, gentle, thirty-eight, and unmarried doesn't have to make a person narrow. She didn't hesitate to hand out the latest fiction to the president of the Methodist missionary society without batting an eye. At times folks did get scandalized by what they read on Miss Malvina's rental shelves, but they didn't seem to be able to stir up much of a row—not like the one caused by the Baptist minister who burned a copy of Hergesheimer's *Cytherea.*

The village was "emancipated" in 1918 and would take a lot of life in the raw. People talked freely about inhibitions and frustrations and other such things, no longer hesitating to know everything that people do and think, inside books and out. The old veil of romance was pulled down, and we looked at everything in the incandescent light of Truth. This was the result of our superior education.—Of course, what could be printed in the *Advocate* was still the old non-libelous, lying rubbish that had kept the paper going for a generation.

I am sure that Miss Malvina never thought about anything very wicked. Though she went on dressing like a college girl, she was obliged to think things that unmarried women of thirty-eight think whether they want to or not. And her thoughts and calculations, I am forced to believe both from observation and for the right I'm assuming to think for her at this moment—her calculations must have included Dr. Boudreau Pemberton, better known locally as "Dr. Budd."

Propinquity, it is said, is a great thing. That's the kind of commonplace you can't always avoid, just as you couldn't avoid seeing Dr. Budd if you went to the library. As you left the stair-well on the second floor, you had to pass right by the door of his office. When the building was bought by the town council from the bank, Dr. Budd went with it like the fixtures. He'd been there a long time and he had no mind to move out ("be damned if he did"), come what may.

His door was always open, and on it was the usual clock face that said, uselessly in the extreme: "Doctor out. Will return at . . ." His gaunt old carcass could be seen distributed between a swivel chair and a desk top as he leant back and propped his feet up to read a newspaper or to gaze endlessly out of a window. He, too, had a shaggy mustache like old Mr. Withers, though it looked more ancient on account of its deep discoloration of amber. When he talked, he did so like a drawl coming away up from his sinuses that made everything he said ridiculous. I avoided him as I'd have avoided the Ancient Mariner. He had no patients, except an occasional Negro who hadn't enough money to lay on the line for one of the younger doctors. Of course, every now and then somebody would say, "Dr. Budd is a mighty good typhoid doctor," though anybody who happened to get the fever promptly called somebody else.

Dr. Budd was a fossil and a fool. But he could not be ignored, for he was a widower who owned a thousand or more acres of the best farm land in the county, had more coupon bonds than he had energy to clip, and belonged to a family sired by Revolutionary captains and Confederate colonels. For a generation every widow and old maid in town had been teased about Dr. Budd. In fact, he was a by-word. When his old Ford runabout wheezed and back-fired up any residential street, the ladies on the piazzas always nodded at each other knowingly about his intent to call on some widow down the block. The Lord only knows exactly how many abortive attempts at courtship he had made since his wife died some years ago. Widows that he had tried to court had passed off the scene in dozens, but Dr. Budd went on. Why nobody married him if only for his money, I cannot say. No doubt every widow and old maid said to herself, "I can get Dr. Budd with the crook of a finger whenever I want him. He's too much of a fool for me to think of doing it now. But if I ever need to think of him, he'll come traveling."

So Dr. Budd was a walking insurance policy against the penniless old age of helpless females, or a bank account that was never drawn on. With all his deadly foolishness and stupidity he was as much a symbol of what is indestructible and deep-rooted as Miss Malvina was of what is fragile and uncertainly underpinned. And they were both together all day long on the second floor of the City Hall with only a thin partition dividing them.

Virtually every day Dr. Budd managed to saunter into the library, slightly dragging his feet in part out of senility and in part out of rakishness.

"Busy?" he intoned. "Dispensing a lot of culture today?"

Miss Malvina didn't do more than barely look over the top of the book that she had grabbed frantically at the sound of his shuffling footsteps in the hall. She dared not do more.

"Good afternoon, Mr. Pemberton," she said. "Can I help you find something?"

"Don't read books," said Dr. Budd. "Can't see any use of the damn things. Newspapers are bad enough."

Around to various shelves he went sniffing like a dog looking for the right tree. Every now and then he pulled out a book, looked at it briefly over his spectacles, and put it back on the shelf haphazardly.

Miss Malvina's neat and orderly soul was outraged.

"You don't have anything by this man Ingersoll or Brann the Iconoclast?" said Dr. Budd, stupidly thinking that these wicked old names would arouse some reaction.

"I believe not," said Miss Malvina, still pretending to read her book.

"Infidels—a passel of infidels. Not fittin' to read," said Dr. Budd, working up a minor tempest.

"We can give you Bunyan's *Pilgrim's Progress* or Sir Thomas Browne's *Religio Medici* or Billy Sunday's sermons," said Miss Malvina. Her tone was as even as her weak voice allowed. She was thinking: "In his office he has several tumors in bottles and a two-headed foetus, and the formaldehyde leaks out. He's bringing the sickening smell in here."

Dr. Budd laughed, half way between a cackle and a sniffle. The laughter was strained through his droopy mustache.

"Young ladies," he said, "ought sometimes to go driving in the open air. It's not good for their health to be hothouse plants."

Miss Malvina made no reply.

Dr. Budd laughed again with a deliberateness suggesting that his laughter was a language all its own. Finally he went back to his office.

Miss Malvina saw the baggy greenish-black suit going down the hall. She visualized the stringy black bow tie against the soiled white shirt, and she saw the heavy gold watch chain suspended vulgarly across the doctor's stomach. She saw him all at once—front, back, and sides—and the vision chilled and fascinated her.

She wished that Dr. Budd did not matter, that he were just an old nuisance sitting among his anatomy charts and his bottled horrors.

"Why should he be more?" she asked herself. "Why? Why? Why?" And she got a little feverish and suffocated by the questioning. In a reasonable amount of time she got herself under control, it is true. But the questioning came again and again. And over a period of time it brought on a dull headache.

It isn't that she didn't know the answers. Most of us really know the answers to a great many questions that we ask and ask and make ourselves sick with asking. Maybe most of our questions do not have answers in a set number of words, but if we ever honestly tried to face them . . . .

"That vixen, Sarah Ferrier, would tear my eyes out!" Miss Malvina said to herself, deriving horror and a temporary kind of satisfaction from the thought, but really evading the truth.

Now Sarah was a married daughter of Dr. Pemberton. There were two other daughters somewhere; but only Sarah lived in town and she was a Tartar: loud-mouthed, vulgar, looking like a meal sack in her clothes, giving no indication that she came from the fine-feathered Pembertons. For a long time people had said that Sarah watched her father like a hawk, scared that somebody would marry the old buzzard and get his money.

Well, why shouldn't Miss Malvina have had the Pemberton place as well as anybody else? The Pembertons themselves had never enjoyed it. "Maymont" was cruelly neglected. If it had been renovated, it would have had real dignity and charm, sitting as it did in a grove of fine pecan trees. In her mind Miss Malvina had painted it gleaming white many times. She had found fresh chintz for the windows and the slipcovers. She had refinished all the old furniture. She had received guests before the fine carved mantel and the huge gold-leaf mirror from which floated little wisps of cobweb. She had seated herself ever so gracefully at the head of the long walnut dining table and caught the glow from the silver candelabra.

There was no doubt that Miss Malvina wanted to be a lady. Life hadn't really played fairly with her. At one time she had had a chance to see the outside world and the promise of doing great things; then she had found herself right back where she started, with a kind of hard shell around her. She had not been embittered, but she had been tantalized. She was coiled up within herself like a watch too tightly wound, always tense and ready to go to pieces inside but somehow ticking on with a beat so regular as to be frantic. And her yeas were not yeas or her nays nays.

In spite of what Miss Malvina told herself, Sarah Ferrier and the smell of formaldehyde were not the real obstacles. There was another one. You would have been able to recognize it only if you had known that Miss Malvina was not as "emancipated" as she maybe pretended that she was and that she didn't let the modern fiction she read get beneath the crust of her consciousness. Actually, Dr. Budd had a rival. We'll call him Jeffrey, not because that is what she really called him but because it is a perfectly credible name for the Victorian young man that he was—right out of an English novel. He was a young man, fully ten years Miss Malvina's junior—a fact which probably bothered her a little. He was a tall, blond, athletic fellow always dressed in immaculate white flannels and a soft snow-white shirt open at the neck. If he smelled of anything, it was delicately of genteel masculine sweat tempered with eau de cologne. He always carried a tennis racquet (properly spelled) and his habitat was a flower-bordered terrace where tea was constantly being served to ladies in flowing gowns and floppy hats. Miss Malvina was, of course, one of the ladies. They all looked ravenously at Jeffrey, but he was irresistibly drawn to Malvina's great wicker chair with the back fanning out like a peacock's tail. He perched gracefully on the arm to kiss Miss Malvina on the lips as she threw her head back in silver laughter.

Now as any amateur psychiatrist knows, it is dangerous to get real and imaginary people mixed. That's where Miss Malvina's trouble lay. She couldn't reconcile Jeffrey and Dr. Budd. If she'd kept one in the world of imagination and the other in the world of fact, the situation might not have been so awful. But she couldn't, and she kept dreaming up a climactic scene. It haunted her idle moments because she half invited it and half fought it off. It ran, I should say, like this:

Dr. Budd comes into the library.

"Busy?" he says. "Earning your pay today?"

She puts down her book and looks up kindly at him.

He walks toward her and she rises to meet him.

"Maybe I can find you something to read," she says gently. "Maybe I can interest you in books."

He takes her soft trembling hand in his gnarled bony ones.

"A pretty young lady like you," he says, "oughtn't to be shut up here like a hothouse plant."

She throws her head back to laugh as she does on the terrace with Jeffrey.

"Could you go for that spin?"

"I'll shut up the place," she says. "It's bright and springlike outside, and it will be an hour or more before the school children will be in or before the ladies have finished their afternoon naps."

"Yes, let's do. I love Maymont."

He takes her in his arms to kiss her, and she closes her eyes. Suddenly he is Jeffrey, ten years younger than she and so very athletic and handsome. Then there is a touch of a rough mustache and the smell of formaldehyde. She represses a scream as one does coming out of a nightmare.

Jeffrey was mighty thin air for an old maid who had to think now about what was coming next in life. It was another great and unfair trial for Miss Malvina.

That's why, maybe, I sometimes found her eyes red from crying when I dropped into the library during the slack time of the afternoon.

VII

PLUM TREE LANE

THE railroad ran through the center of town for the simplest of reasons: that is, the railroad was there before the town was. At first there was only an "X-road" (as the *Advocate* graphically put it) which, having got a station, acquired houses and stores around it and alongside the tracks. The town limits ran one mile to the north, south, east, and west of the station, making an area of four square miles (as the most elementary of mathematics figures it), though at least three of these were merely fields and woods. Along either side of the tracks ran a dirt road that was eventually paved, but not for over half a century after the railroad came through. It was called with undeserved grandeur, Railroad Avenue.

For years the last street to the west of the station— and less than three hundred yards from it—was Plum Tree Lane, so called because along it at one point ran the plum orchard of a retired pharmacist locally styled "Dr." Riddle. The street started just a block north of the tracks in a wooded area, or informal park, called Hunter's Grove and ran a little over half a mile south until it wound up (symbolically?) in the town cemetery. It was lined with fine elm and oak trees (many of the latter being willow oaks); and, like all the other streets in the village, it remained unpaved for the duration of my childhood.

The *terminus a quo* and the *terminus ad quem* of the street (in terms that I acquired somewhat later than my high-school Latin class) I measured memorably one day when I was about fourteen. The occasion was the interruption of a doubles game that I was playing one summer day on the Hamiltons' tennis court on the edge of Hunter's Wood. In the midst of the game, up rode Elise Wesson on a fine, brown hunter. She was using not a side-saddle but a regular one, which seemed to work rather well with her split riding skirt, topped by a fluffy white blouse and a pert little feathered brown hat. Everybody stopped playing tennis, as people usually stopped everything when Elise appeared. And somebody suggested that she allow each of us to take his turn at riding the beast. She agreed, and I was elected unanimously to have the first go. Knowing that I was not a good horseman, I showed the proper reluctance, not to mention the proper generosity, in offering my turn to one of the others. But I soon discovered that my election was not one that could honorably be refused. So amid cheers, I mounted. Taking the bridle in hand, I gave what I considered the go-forward nudge with my feet in the horse's flanks. The result was magic—or worse. The animal took off as if it were a plane shot from the deck of an aircraft carrier—or, in a more appropriate figure to the time borrowed from "The Diverting History of John Gilpin,"—

> So like an arrow swift he flew,
> Shot by an archer strong;
> So did he fly—which brings me to
> The middle of my song

that is, of the poet's song, not mine; for I had much space to cover yet. In fact, away we went down the street, across the railroad track just ahead of a puffing freight train (just like a Mack Sennett comedy), and on down the street past Trigman's Corner, past the plum orchard, past Masterman's Corner, across the Columbia-Augusta highway—with me standing in the stirrups, as jockeys do, and pulling for dear life on the bridle, quite unlike any knowledgeable jockey. Then down a hill we went and up again until we ran through the gate of the cemetery. Luckily the gate was not closed; otherwise there would certainly have been a disastrous jump—not for the horse who could do it but for me who could not follow him. On among the grave stones we flew until I finally managed to stop Pegasus by heading him into a stone of noble proportions. Here I turned him around—but not to my advantage; for once he saw that he was headed back he flew as fast as he had come, if not faster, with me attempting in the utmost desperation to stay attached to him. Of the end of the luckless ride of the linen-draper John Gilpin from London to Edmonton and Ware and back, the poetic account runs as follows:

> Nor stopped he until where he had got up
> He did again get down.

Nor stopped I; and I did get down where I had got up, but not of my own will and accord. When the horse was just about to head into the backstop of the tennis court, he made a neat turn. Without knowing how I got there, I found myself on my back on the ground watching hooves neatly sidestep me while their owner nuzzled his nose into the shoulder of his mistress, doubtless expecting a lump of sugar as a reward for his dazzling performance. For me it was an ignominious occasion. I never really trusted a horse again.

In the whole stretch of Plum Tree Lane there were not many families because each house was set in several acres of land. Across the railroad track lived the Hamiltons in a spacious cream-colored two-story house with a turret seeming to arise from the surrounding porches. Across the way was a big green bungalow in which one of the several Collins families lived. On a street perpendicular to the Lane and behind the Collins house was the extensive acreage of the Wesson place and the smaller acreage of the Morrells—all of which seemed to be only an extension of our street.

On the south side of the tracks on the two corners lived the Trigmans and the largest Collins family, both in rambling two-story houses with generous lawns, magnolia trees, and scuppernong arbors. Mrs. Trigman was a widow who for a number of years had run a hotel that, according to an advertisement in the 1902 *Advocate,* offered room and board for two dollars a day. (Her customers came from drummers, who were practically the only people who patronized "hotels" in small towns.) But by the time I came along, the house was simply a residence, except for the fact that every year a school teacher or two might be taken in to board. Mr. Elbert Collins, who lived across the street and who was a close relative of Mrs. Trigman, was a merchant like my father, but on a considerably larger scale. He had to be, for he had had two wives and had produced a family of eight. In addition to general merchandise, he offered buggies, wagons, and mules; moreover, he bought and sold cotton.

Next to the Trigmans on our side of the street was a section of lawn that was later to be the site of a house in which my Aunt Clarina lived. Across the street from us lived the family of Fred Collins in a tall, green, gabled house that looked a little like a great bird with wings poised to take off. Next to that was what we called "the brown house," which had a number of tenants during my childhood: first, old Miss Eliza Collins who lived there with a niece and took boarders, then the Bartons, then the Greenfields, and so on. Next to us lived my cousins, Bradford and Sarah Evans, in another sprawling white turreted house with surrounding porch, a type of architecture that was locally stylish in the early decades of the century. The place had a fine lawn and a well-kept orchard, as well as a tennis court which was in the summer an outdoor social center for the street. Cousin Bradford was another merchant, who added to his establishment for general merchandise a funeral parlor with a flourishing trade in caskets. Finally on the corner next to the highway lived the Mastermans in another rambling, gabled house almost invisible because it had a surrounding garden heavily planted in shrubs, trees, vines, and flowers. Mr. Masterman was a banker and cotton broker and was generally conceded to be the richest man in town. Certainly, with his well-brushed silver hair, his carefully clipped mustache, and his freshly pressed clothes he gave the impression of being a man of fashion and distinction. His wife, retiring though she was, also gave the impression of being equally fashionable. The Mastermans had a carriage that was at times driven by a black coachman (who in time became their chauffeur); and they were the first people in town to have a permanent summer home in the North Carolina mountains, though some other local families leased places in the mountains for all or part of the summer. So far as our area was concerned at the time, there was no prestige attached to owning a house at the beach. Such houses were only for coastal residents who were not rich enough to be able to flee the malaria and mosquitoes of the Low Country for summer residences in Saluda or Flat Rock in North Carolina.

So far as the southernmost section of Plum Tree Lane is concerned, it is hardly necessary to cross the highway and go down the street toward the cemetery. The white families who lived there were entirely respectable, and the black families who lived close to the cemetery gate were the most substantial in town. But they only occasionally impinged upon my consciousness or took any substantial part in the goings-on in the "best" part of the Lane.

Turning back to the part of the street north of the railroad tracks and especially the adjunct to it, my account must include something that was very much a part of my childhood experience—in fact, a kind of second home: the Wesson place.

Since my Barclay grandparents died long before I was born, I had little notion about them. I may have seen a picture or two, but my impressions and my interest were both vague. Three of my father's sisters—Aunt Allie, Aunt Clarina, and Aunt Tessie—often were in evidence; but my father's brothers I never knew, except the youngest one named Uncle Alexander, a nice, wiry little man who lived in Beddington, some twenty miles away, and who several times a year arrived by the early morning train to spend Sunday with us. We always got on the train on the Fourth of July to visit him for a pit barbecue that he annually staged for relatives and friends in a little grove near his house, where tables had been set up with containers of wonderful barbecue hash, as well as great bowls of cole slaw and scores of watermelons cut in halves and quarters. I liked Uncle Alexander very much.

I regret that I did not know Uncle David. He started out as the telegraph operator and ticket agent at the depot and eventually became president of the First National Bank of Bayesville. Aunt Elise was his widow; and since she was Elise Wesson's grandmother, she served as a kind of grandmother image for me—on the paternal side. She had two sons and a daughter, all of whom were grown when I was old enough to know them. Basil, who like his brother Hunt had gone to Richmond College, had got a job with a brokerage firm in Atlanta after his graduation. I knew him as an immaculately groomed bachelor wearing a pince-nez on a black grosgrain ribbon and looking very much like a man about town. Hunt, tall and ruggedly good looking, was married and living in Charleston as a minor official in the Atlantic Coast Line Railway. Anna Maude, the daughter, had gone to Brenau Conservatory to study the piano. Talented, pretty, and overindulged (like her daughter), she had made a good catch in Dr. Albert Wesson, whose father was one of the richest planters in the county.

A year before I was born, Elise Wesson had arrived on the scene, and slightly later contracts were let on a house that Aunt Elise and the young Wessons planned as something that would be head and shoulders above everything else in the community in luxury and in elegance—as it eventually became pretty close to being. The architect, whoever he was, managed to avoid both the Greek revival house that had long served as a symbol of the moonlight-and-magnolia South and the Victorian turreted house that had only recently become too popular unlike either Tara or the Pavilion at Brighton (so often reproduced in magazines). He leaned toward the Georgian or maybe the Palladian, erecting a rectangular cream-colored frame house with a restrained one-story portico in front and an uncovered terrace. One dignified dormer window in the slate roof, a graceful bay on one side, and a conservatory or sun parlor on the other kept the lines of the house from being too severe. The surrounding gardens were cleanly defined by low neatly clipped privet hedges. Brick gateposts with lanterns and heavy iron chains led to a circular graveled driveway, bordered by small arbor vitae. The lawn was a lush green carpet summer and winter; and the planting included boxwood, clumps of hydrangeas and Banksia roses, and, most importantly, plants like banana shrub and tea olive that gave off exquisite perfume on warm summer days and nights. A cutting garden screened by a high hedge was just beyond the lawn and attached to it was a greenhouse of considerable size which provided flowers and plants for the house in all seasons of the year.

The house was not less impressive inside. The double front doors under a small fanlight opened into a vestibule that in turn led into a large reception hall with a stairway sweeping grandly up to a platform and beyond to the second floor. The drawing room was set off from the hall by a pair of delicately fluted wooden columns on either side of a wide opening, curtained with velvet of rich dark brown on the hall side and dark green on the drawing room side. The dining room gained a majestic look because of its bay window. Then there were the music room and the sun parlor, both spacious. Some of the furniture was inherited—like the large and small rosewood Victorian sofas covered with black horsehair, prickly to back and bottom in the summertime and very hard at any time to sit on without slipping. Other pieces were the result of Anna Maude's foraging the countryside for antiques or her visits to Biggs in Richmond where the best Chippendale reproductions were. The rugs were Oriental; the carpets came from W. & J. Sloane. Gold-framed Audubon prints hung on the walls. The china was Haviland. The flat silver was light old coin silver, inherited and collected, or heavy stuff imported from Gorham. The crystal was either antique pressed or the popular American cut glass. A Tiffany shade covered the light bulbs over the dining table. In spite of the fact that the house was equipped with steam heating, a rarity in our village at the time, each room had a handsome fireplace with a carved classic mantle and shining brass andirons, screen, and fender. Everything was formal and precise—except the sun parlor, which was, as it should have been, bright and casual in chintz and wicker and growing plants. Aunt Elise and Anna Maude had studied the magazines and the books on interior decoration well. And they more than knew what they wanted—they got it.

It was in the sun parlor that Aunt Elise sat in the mornings and in the late afternoons, presiding over the household with the numerous outbuildings and gardens around it, two farms in the country called Flat Rock and the Stuckman Place, and anything else she could think of presiding over. Menus for the day, household accounts, bills for seed and fertilizer for the farms—all were referred to her. Although I never knew when she had time to use it, she had a secretary desk in her bedroom where she kept her accounts and a diary in which she set down as much as she could about her daily life and that of the town. Unfortunately, this valuable document is now lost.

Always dressed in black silk with a white lace collar held up by whalebone stays and always sitting in a high-backed wicker rocking chair with a pillow beneath her feet and a slender black, silver-tipped cane at her side, she needed only a lace cap to look like Queen Victoria as she might have been played by George Arliss. Anna Maude and young Elise both called her "Mamma" and responded to her with "Ma'm" as one does to royalty. Mary Wayne, the cook, and Jake Layton, the general factotum (and John Brown to Aunt Elise's Victoria), approached her with quiet deference. Dr. Wesson was never obsequious. A chronically good-natured, sunny, and mild-tempered man, he settled for always calling his mother-in-law "Mrs. Barclay" and never crossing her, giving the impression of being glad never to have to bother about domestic details.

As for me, I thought Aunt Elise was dour. She rarely smiled a good full-faced smile; and when she laughed, she could produce little more than a dry cackle that one could have set a match to. Being a good deal younger and of an entirely different stamp from her sister-in-law, my mother did not approve of her—especially her pretense to grandeur. "She isn't so fine as she sets up to be," I was told once in something less than strict confidence. "Her mother was a seamstress, and one of her sisters ran away with a man—to New Orleans." (Ah, what a skeleton in the closet!) I didn't wholly approve of Aunt Elise either, but she liked me and I felt that I could not be disloyal. Besides I was not fully aware of the low social status of seamstresses or of the enormity of carnal sins. So I made no comment. I am afraid that I wondered whether my mother might not be just a bit jealous of Aunt Elise's luxury as she was of Aunt Clarina's beauty.

I, of course, reveled in the luxury of the Wesson place. In the summer when I was not "boarding" with Elise, I was frequently asked to have the midday meal at the big house—for which I knew enough to scrub and brush myself properly, certain that I'd be served stylishly by Mary Wayne, sometimes assisted by a girl named Minnie. But most of all I liked being invited to breakfast on winter mornings before Elise and I went to school. I knew that in the butler's pantry was a crock of buckwheat batter always "working" and that in the kitchen on the big, hooded range was a soapstone from which came an enchanting series of brown cakes dotted with holes into which could be poured melted butter and ribbon-cane syrup. On the side would be hominy grits and spicy, peppery sausages or fried ham. The coffee (I was never denied it after I became old enough to demand it) was brewed like ours from coffee beans roasted and ground daily. With cream in it, it turned almost red and had a special winey flavor.

I was well aware where sausages and hams came from, for I had been on hand as early as I was allowed to go to the hog-butcherings at Aunt Elise's—usually on a tingling cold weekend in November. Almost all other domestic animals except hogs were raised on the premises. On the edge of the acreage was a beautiful gray barn with a gambrel roof that had a second floor large enough for a ball room even when the fodder and hay were stored there. Cows, horses, buggies, wagons, and farm machinery and eventually motor cars were below. Next to the barnyard was a yard with chickens, turkeys, and geese, with maybe a guinea hen now and then. (Once there was even a peacock.) The hogs, however, were raised on the farms. The reason they were not butchered there is simple. Aunt Elise wanted to see that it was done as she wanted it done and as she knew it ought to be done. Besides, there was plenty of space on her ample grounds.

So on the appointed day, determined by the *Farmer's Almanac* and doubtless the moon, the tenants came with their wagons loaded with the hogs killed and covered with blood-stained white cloths. Awaiting them was a festival scene with big black iron pots and fires burning under them, and with stands and tables provided with knives for cutting up the carcasses, as well as grinders and other implements for converting the pork into sausage and the hog jowl and liver into liver pudding. Women and men in white aprons were soon working all over the area.

Since the event usually came on a weekend, John Morrell, Elise, and I could be expected to be on hand. If Saturday happened not to be the day, we rushed home from school as soon as we could on whatever day in order not to miss the afternoon activities. Paradoxically, I, who could not bear to see a chicken killed, felt no qualms at the butchering affair. The best part was that nobody shooed us off, though at times in order to assure that we were not being too nosey Aunt Elise would summon us to her throne-like chair where she sat swathed in black woolen shawls, wearing one of Dr. Wesson's old felt hats pulled down over her ears, and directing the operations with her cane almost as a maestro conducts an orchestra. And by imperial order we were given clean white bladders to blow up like balloons and deliciously crisp and dry rinds from the kettles where lard was being rendered. (Crackling bread would come later!)

Everything, I was sure, would eventually be equitably distributed among tenants and landlord, and all that part due to Aunt Elise would be carefully packed and ticketed for storage in the big square stone smokehouse that she had built and that she always kept festooned with links of sausage and liver pudding and hams and shoulders hanging for curing.

The fun that we had at butchering time was likely to stay longer in my memory than my observation of the other types of social life distinctly unbucolic that went on in the big house, which Anna Maude loved to use for musicals, and "dress-up" receptions, and large card parties—all stylishly conducted. These Elise and I could witness only through the banisters of the front stairway.

Leaving my own household out of consideration, the Lane was, indeed, the most social area in town, especially in the summertime. Somebody was always importing out-of-town visitors, girls from finishing schools, boys from colleges, or relatives from neighboring towns. Clarence Trigman and his sisters, together with the young Collinses, married and unmarried, seemed always to be having parties. On almost any weekend from May to September one of the lawns on the street was strung up with Japanese lanterns, studded with chairs and benches deployed for "progressive conversation," and marked off with aisles for "promenading." Inside one of the houses there was usually dancing, either to the music of a phonograph or a piano, which a variety of people could play acceptably. To me Clarence Trigman was the star performer of ragtime. When he addressed himself to the old upright Beckstein and played something like the "Turkey Trot," surely nobody in the world could have been better. His sister Carrie was also accomplished. She was particularly good with waltzes like those from *The Merry Widow* and *The Pink Lady,* and she gave a brilliant rendering of "Over the Waves"—like a pianola.

Fred Collins and I usually managed to "crash" the parties—though "crash" is hardly the word. Rather we haunted the fringes of the affairs, watching the dancers through windows, peering at the promenaders through hedges, repressing giggles at what we saw going on in dark nooks, and emerging periodically to raid the table that held the punch bowl and the cookie trays.

Fred's family, like John Morrell's, I regarded as being glamorous. His statuesque mother was stylish rather than pretty. Warm and affectionate, she had a low-pitched, throaty voice that I considered most becoming. Fred's sister, Francesca, who was three years older than he, was another of the beautiful girls in our neighborhood who assumed a gently protective attitude toward me and for whom I developed a lasting affection. Fred's father, a man in his early thirties, who was good looking in a curly-headed Irish way, was a traveling salesman whom I saw infrequently. What I remember about him most vividly was that when he was at home he would sit on the front porch all day long drinking ice water from a pitcher on a table beside him. At the time, I did not understand the reason. Then one day I learned that he had died (he had been baptized a Catholic and I saw through the window the candles burning around his coffin), and I overheard older people say in hushed voices what a pity it was that such an attractive and affable young man should have allowed liquor to take him to his grave.

The Collinses on the corner and the Trigmans had such large family connections, and interconnections, that activities in and around both these houses were always lively, even when now and then there had to be a funeral. Of the eight Collinses at least five were much older than I, but three were close enough in age to move in my circle of play: Dewey, who was big, friendly, coarse, and wayward, did all those daring things like smoking cigarettes behind the barn and drinking vanilla extract that made him both wicked and masculine. Flo was good-hearted but gawky and never seemed to brush her teeth. Leta was the pick of the lot. Frail in a nice elfin kind of way, she was outgoing, sweet, and very bright. I liked her best.

After the death of Fred's father, his family moved in to live with Grandmother Trigman, and the Badhams moved into the green house, bringing two more boys into the neighborhood: Roderick, a tall, handsome, and slightly brassy lad about Dewey's age, and Damon, a pallid, moody, and imaginative boy only a little older than Fred and I.

When the second Mrs. Elbert Collins died in childbirth, Miss Eliza moved in to take care of her widowed brother's family, and into the brown house moved a grandfather of some of the Collins children, a retired Baptist minister and his old-maid daughter. The neighborhood was changing, and the complexity of relationships grew. Then there came a different kind of change. Cousin Bradford sold his business and bought a clothing store in Augusta. So he and my jolly Cousin Sarah sold their house to the Gerstons, a well-to-do Jewish merchant family with a young daughter and son.

The religious affiliations of the people on our block were inclined to be as complicated as the family connections. The Trigmans and the Collinses were an incomprehensible mixture of Catholics and Baptists. Most of the Catholics were women, but not all. But the women who were Catholic married Baptist men, and the men who were Catholics married Baptist or Presbyterian women. There was no consistency in adhering to the Faith, a fact which must have baffled and annoyed the Catholic priests who on occasion came from neighboring towns to administer various sacraments. My own background was Lutheran, Baptist, and Episcopalian. But my Episcopalian relatives had in the absence of their own church gone largely over to the Baptists. What Presbyterians there were in town had had to make a choice between the Methodists and the Baptists, for who could live respectably in a small South Carolina town in the early decades of the century without being a member of some church? Not only social propriety but credit depended upon such membership.

By the time I came along the great schism that had existed earlier between the Methodists and the Baptists had almost disappeared. At one time there had been so much antagonism that Baptists would not engage in business dealings with Methodists and vice versa, and two separate schools had to be set up so that the immersionists and the sprinklers could be kept apart. The bitterness vanished, but the rivalry continued—especially among the ladies who always tried to outdo their counterparts in the rival sect in their church suppers and bazaars, each sect claiming social superiority over the other.

Now that we had a Baptist minister and a Jewish family on our block, we were ready to become really ecumenical. After all, the Hamiltons who lived across the tracks were Methodists; and they had become perfectly acceptable. Certainly, little religious distinction was made among the children, who Catholic, Jewish, Baptist, and Methodist alike went together at times to the same Sunday School and attended the same meetings of the Sunbeams, the Royal Ambassadors, or Christian Endeavor, especially when ice cream was served.

The Gerstons added a special flavor to the neighborhood. They were different and yet they were not very different. Mr. Gerston was a neat and pleasant man with a certain crispness that suggested efficiency and sharpness in business. People said admiringly that he had come from Russia to this country with only a pack on his back. (I knew from Horatio Alger how people like him made good.) Mrs. Gerston was a dark luscious Mediterranean beauty who was soft and affable and given to the most delicious malapropisms. Rebekah, the daughter, was blonde, and quiet. Sam, much younger, was a dark, handsome child. Both had the best of manners. I never considered the family in a religious light. They certainly appeared to be far from anything that could be considered orthodox in their faith. I do remember hearing something said about a circumcision ceremony when Sam was born. But I never saw a rabbi at the Gerston house as I saw an occasional priest at the Trigmans', and there was no occasion yet for a bar mitzvah. But I did have matzoth from the Gerstons during the Passover season and gefilte fish and maybe even a bit of wine. The only thing that I can say is that I liked their potato pancakes best of all and that, if other things were cooked with schmaltz rather than butter, they were all first-rate.

Our Reverend Mr. Barton was a kind and gentle old man, deaf as a post, whose religion was doubtless as deep as it was unobtrusive. The real power was his spinster daughter, Miss Millie, who not only ran the house for him but who was the self-appointed moral censor for the town. She was about Aunt Allie's age and they both taught Sunday School, but for piety Aunt Allie could not hold a candle to Miss Millie. Everybody was mortally afraid of her and eager to hide from her any trace of his or her most venial sin. Many a deck of cards vanished as if by magic from a bridge table on a summer front porch when one of the players sensed the presence of Miss Millie coming down the street. The typical story that ran about the town was the one about Miss Millie's reprimand to one of her Collins nieces for going late to a bridge party "for refreshments." When the niece protested that she had not in any way engaged in a card game there but had merely eaten the frozen fruit salad and beaten biscuits served to the guests, Miss Millie replied, "Yes, but you sinned by going to the house of sin."

The "house of sin" in this instance happened to be that of a cousin of mine. Our house would have been one, too (but for another reason), if my mother had extended to Miss Millie her custom of serving blackberry wine and fruit cake to afternoon callers. My mother, being firm in her own convictions, rather appreciated Miss Millie and she was not afraid of her censure. Yet she had better taste and sense than deliberately to offend; so Miss Millie got iced or hot tea with tea cakes, according to season. Whether Miss Millie ever propagandized for the Women's Christian Temperance Union in our parlor, I do not know; but I should not be surprised if she did, for she had all the zeal, if little of the violence, of Carry Nation. My mother as a staunch non-joiner apparently resisted enlistment in the cause.

I remember one impingement that involved me and in which I found myself, if not entirely willingly, on the side of Miss Millie against my mother. One day at Sunday School Miss Millie produced little white cards for her class to sign, along with little bits of white ribbon and a collection of straight pins for attaching the ribbon to our clothing after we had affixed our signatures. The cards very likely bore the text "Wine is a mocker; strong drink is raging," for it was a favorite of Miss Millie and we had all chanted it in class a number of times. The pledge on the card had been read to us, and it was an awful vow never, no never to let wine or liquor touch our lips. Since I had already turned against wine because of the castor oil I had had to drink in it and thus remembered only the disagreeable aspects of the liquid, I did not have much trouble in signing.

Feeling all noble and pious, I went home to Sunday dinner. Out came the standard baked hen with all the trimmings. Then to top off the meal appeared one of those lucious and seductive desserts that my mother could produce in the twinkling of an eye. I have forgotten whether it was Floating Island or Tipsy Cake or Charlotte Russe. But it was flavored with wine, very definitely flavored with wine. This alarming recognition struck me when the first spoonful was on the way down. Filled with horror that I was breaking my freshly made and solemn vow, I paused, grabbed my napkin, and pushed away from the table, somehow managing to point to my white ribbon as I did so. I was not called back. My parents allowed me to go away quietly and meditate about my fall from grace. I hasten to say, however, that I did not forever turn down the best desserts of the house because wine had been used to flavor them.

My friends and I also played cards—simple games at first like Smut (so called because the loser got his face blacked with soot from the back of a fireplace), Rummy, and Set-Back ("High, Low, Jack, and Game"). But we usually played upstairs in somebody's house or on a porch or under an arbor so well concealed by vines from Miss Millie's piercing eye that she could not stop us, possibly menacingly waving as she descended upon us the parasol that she usually carried. (This latter prospect, to be sure, was entirely in our imagination; for with all her zeal for her causes and for all her moral severity, I never saw her act in any way that was not completely ladylike.) In time, we finally thought that we had found a way to get around Miss Millie openly—that is by playing Flinch or Rook, with cards that had numbers on them rather than the hated pictures and colors instead of spades, hearts, diamonds, and clubs. But to Miss Millie they were still cards, and the ruse did not completely work.

After several years Mr. Barton died, and Miss Millie went to live with a sister in another part of town. So we felt a certain amount of freedom from being visited by Divine Wrath for the sins that Miss Millie thought so mortal. We then did worse things than playing cards, like snitching plums from Dr. Riddle's orchard in season. And sometimes we got caught, as I did one day, when, having snitched one of the big luscious purple things on a dare from Fred, Dr. Riddle materialized from under a tree—and just at the moment when I had crammed the fruit into my mouth. As in the ancient story of Adam's apple, the sinful plum lodged in my throat. I received a stiff lecture, but because of the tears in my eyes— induced by the choking as well as by fright—I was mercifully let off without a threat of being reported to my parents. Dr. Riddle was the superintendent of our Sunday School and at the assembly he always kneeled down at the front of the auditorium when he prayed to the Almighty, as he did frequently and long; so I knew that he was fully as saintly as Miss Millie. But on this occasion he acted with the kind of charity of which, I felt, all Baptists were not capable. Had Miss Millie caught me, I was sure, my parents would have known; and I should have had one of those stinging switchings which my father, though in most instances indulgent, could perform on occasions that seemed to him proper—especially when I was being trained to separate right from wrong. "Never touch anything that doesn't belong to you" had always been one of his ringing admonitions—and that definitely applied to our neighbors' peaches, plums, apples and pears, which we all found so tempting.

For children there were, anyhow, plenty of unsinful amusements on the lane. Down beyond Trigman's corner, for example, were the trains, which were always fascinating, especially the passenger trains. Even the freight trains were not dull. On a summer day it was fun to perch on a pile of crossties, as if on a grandstand, and watch the engines shift the box cars on the sidings that led to the cotton seed oil mill, the fertilizer plant, and the saw mill, casually shedding cars to move along the tracks by themselves until they banged into another group of cars or were expertly brought to a standstill by a brakeman who emerged from nowhere.

The passenger trains were more interesting simply because you could see people in them. And people were forever coming and going, even if they were just going between Columbia and Augusta or Fredonia and Johnston—all indulging in the great mystery of travel. We waved to them as they went by, and they waved back—often out of open windows. And waving to engineers was the greatest sport of all. It occurred to me that one of the finest things in life would be to know an engineer, even though I might not be able to be one. Elise Wesson, naturally, contrived to do just that. She began waving to an engineer on the eight o'clock morning train and continued to do so for several months. He waved back. Then one day Elise had Mary Wayne make up a fine box lunch—with sausage biscuits, sandwiches, and lots of cake— and Jake took it down to deliver it at the station. I remember the engineer very well from seeing him go by. He was a fat man with yellowish white hair beneath his blue cap and a walrus mustache above his coveralls.

The triumph was that the engineer wrote a thank-you note and dropped it off at the station the next day for somebody to take to Elise. So she knew an engineer by name—Mr. Westmoreland—and could claim him as her own. I waved to him, too, but he didn't know me. Therefore, once again Elise was ahead of me.

Anyway, Fred, John, and I waved to Mr. Westmoreland and other engineers and firemen and brakemen, and we wove our fantasies about the engineers and the people that they transported on their trains, providing a language as all children do out of the sounds made by the engines and of the hum of the telegraph wires that ran along the tracks. When our trains got past the commonplace I-think-I-can-I-think-I-can type of chugging and puffing necessary to leaving the station, they came by Trigman's Corner saying something peculiarly descriptive: namely, "Black and dusty, going to Augusty." And they repeated it with ever quickening rhythm and diminishing sound as they disappeared down the track into a little black dot on the horizon.

Trains were the attraction of Trigman's Corner; automobiles, of Masterman's. So we had only to go from one to the other to vary our amusement.

In my birth year some forty-nine new makes of automobiles came onto the market. Such a surprising figure suggests that the idea of the "horseless carriage" was beginning to catch on in a big way and that many people were engaged in a new kind of gold rush, frantically trying to get into a market whose future dimensions were as yet only dimly foreseen. It is interesting to note that of all the new names on the list of 1906, only one has persisted: Pontiac. But it was some years before an automobile could be purchased closer to Bayesville than Columbia or Augusta. The old *Advocate* of 1902 that I have been quoting indicates the existence of livery stables but not garages. Fifteen years later a complete revolution had taken place; thus the Town Directory of 1917 listed four garages with agencies for the Maxwell, Velie, Overland, Ford, Paige, Reo, Franklin, and Chevrolet. Moreover, three people offered automobiles "for hire"—in a limited way, taxi service. Livery stables were plainly extinct.

I am not sure that in 1906 anybody in town had a car. For a long time it did not occur to me that the horse and buggy era was not with us to stay. Certainly on the Columbia-Augusta highway (later U.S. 1), the traffic for the first decade of the century was largely horse- or mule-drawn: carts, wagons, carriages, buggies, surreys, and even an occasional racing trap. There were also mule-back and horse-back riders. The most colorful of the latter was distinguished old Colonel Wesson, who with flowing white mustachios and goatee under a wide-brimmed gray hat, rode in with precise, straight-backed dignity from his plantation nine miles away. There were some other smartly dressed riders, too, but none so fine as the colonel.

One of my earliest memories of a car (though I cannot date it) is that of a red Ford runabout, high off the ground and topless, that belonged to a physician named Dr. Twitchell. The second is that of a black Winton touring car that the Bayeses drove in from their place just beyond the edge of town.

In 1906, and in the years immediately following, automobiles were expensive, especially the better ones, and only the richest people in our community could afford them at first. Advertisements in the universally read *Literary Digest* quoted the Pope-Toledo four-cylinder touring car at $2,800, a figure exactly matched by the Cadillac and Winton. Nevertheless, one might have a Franklin five passenger touring model with tonneau for $1,550, a Rambler Surrey for $1,350, or even a Cadillac side-entrance model for $950—all prices F.O.B. Fords may have been cheaper, but the era of the mass-produced automobile within the reach of almost all was still several years off.

When my playmates and I began automobile "collecting" (and about the same time that we began collecting cards with pictures of baseball players from the cigarette packs), a car or two a day might be our limit. They were all carefully noted and identified as to model and make. As time went on and traffic increased, the game became considerably more interesting and complicated. Aiken and Augusta, both between thirty and forty-odd miles away, were established winter resorts; and although most of the winter residents chose to come down by the reasonably luxurious trains of the time, some were beginning to motor down and more were sending their cars down by their chauffeurs. Since most of these vehicles had to pass Masterman's Corner in order to get to their destinations, on a banner afternoon in late fall or early winter, one might be able to log a Cadillac or a Packard, or even a Peerless or a Pierce-Arrow with license plates indicating that they were from New York or New Jersey. The most special of all would be a Stanley or White steamer. I saw only one of these in my whole automobile-collecting career. Somehow we always had hopes (or rather fantasies) of seeing our hero, Barney Oldfield, come by in his racer, raising dust like forty; but we never did.

As time went on we reaped the rewards of the fad of "boosting." It worked in this way: The Columbia Chamber of Commerce would put on the road, with Augusta as its objective, a fleet of cars all decorated and bearing signs that read "Boost Columbia" and other similar things. This caravan would stop at small towns all along the way to disseminate propaganda. But since Masterman's Corner was close to being midway in the course, the stop lasted longer than the rest. Here the ladies married to members of our own Chamber of Commerce—the Bayesville "boosters"—had set up tables covered with gaily colored tissue paper and festooned with streamers and balloons, from which, floating like cotton balls in their fluffy white summer dresses, they served coffee, lemonade, chicken salad and tomato sandwiches, and assorted cakes to the visitors. It was, indeed, a festive occasion. Then a month or more later the Augusta boosters would come along and the whole affair would be repeated. The Bayesville boosters, I understood, even made forays of their own, though never to such large towns as Columbia and Augusta. Since these occasions did not involve Masterman's Corner, they were of no interest to me.

I never understood what good our kind of hospitality did anyway, especially since the boosters were plainly urging our people to shop in Columbia and Augusta rather than at home. But everybody seemed to have fun, and certainly I did. The days of the boosters not only produced a splendid picnic and an automobile-collecting bonanza, but it was also good as a people-watching experience. The women were in every sense romantic in their long buff-colored linen dusters and large hats covered with veils and tied under beautiful chins, just like the drawings of Howard Chandler Christy in the *Saturday Evening Post*. And the men looked highly sporting in their own dusters, tweedy caps, and big black-rimmed goggles.

The extension of the world of Plum Tree Lane, indeed, was always welcome, and it was especially so on a warm summer day.

VIII

OLD HOMEPLACE

MY mother's "old homeplace," as she always called it, was named "Baxter." Just how the house got the name I was never quite certain, though the assumption is that it came from the family that had the original royal grant for the land. Not only was Baxter a house; it was a post office. And it also had a railroad flag stop—a little yellow shed perched on a mound of sand fringed with a few miserable scrub oaks; and it had a sign on it that said not "Baxter" but "Keller," which was the name of my mother's family.

It was at the flag stop that we usually arrived. Baxter or Keller was only five miles from Bayesville and could be easily reached by horse and buggy. But since we did not have that kind of transportation, we went by train— sometimes on Sundays or on holidays when my father did not have to tend his store, though most often on week days when my mother and I went by ourselves.

The train ride was for me the most enjoyable part of the visit. Except for infrequent trips to Columbia when my mother took me shopping with her or to Augusta to visit my Evans cousins after they moved there, my experience with travel was limited. So a train ride of any sort was an adventure. The visit to Baxter I considered as quite the opposite. In fact, when my mother announced that a trip was in prospect, I usually tried to find some excuse for not going: the Morrells were going to have a picnic, Anna Maude Wesson had invited me to spend the day with Elise, and so on. Bayesville was hardly urban, but Baxter was "country" and a different world—a fact which made me uncomfortable. My mother did not appreciate my attitude in the slightest.

The train stop was on a spur line designed to join the Columbia-Augusta Southern Railway line with the Columbia-Charleston route at a junction called Berry, only about twenty miles from Bayesville. A separate company called the Carolina Midland Railway originally operated the branch, its only rolling equipment being a tiny engine and two coaches: the first divided between baggage and a passenger compartment for Negroes and the second being a coach for whites.

The whole idea seemed to make very little sense, for the convenience of going to Charleston via Berry rather than via Columbia was minimal; and the route slashed through a most unproductive and sparsely populated region of pine barrens and sand hills, salubrious to consumptives, as the area around Aiken was early thought to be, but to hardly anybody else—especially since agriculture was likely to be mostly hard-scrabble. The operation was closer to that of the Toonerville Trolley of the cartoon than anything else I can think of. The "Midlin," as it was called, had a personality all its own; and when I saw it sitting on a siding near the Bayesville station, as it did in the evenings, with a little smoke and steam lazily issuing from it, I felt that it was a living thing—maybe like a great St. Bernard dog that could be patted. Almost everything about the schedule was purely casual. The conductor knew everybody who traveled on the train or who greeted him at the various stations; and pauses along the route for conversation or for picking berries would not have been surprising. The passenger coach, with ornate but faded decoration inside, had the usual reversible seats covered with prickly red mohair. It was lit when it needed to be with kerosene lamps in highly bossed brass holders. The windows were wide open in the summertime, and cinders were everywhere.

As a rule, we were not met at the Keller flag stop, for we did not always bother to announce our visit in advance. But on the way back, we were formally conducted to the little yellow shed. It was the hospitable thing to do; then, too, somebody had to flag the train. This procedure was always romantic. In the summer when it was still daylight at five-thirty or six, we would wait for the appearance of the train on the horizon—a tiny dot with a little plume of black smoke, both of which became larger and larger as the engine rocked along toward us. Then as the headlight and cow-catcher became clearly discernible, one of my uncles would get out a large white handkerchief, stand athwart the track on the side of the engineer, and wave back and forth— daringly I felt. A toot from the whistle would announce that we had been sighted and that passage was assured. In the winter when dark came at five o'clock, the signal was made, even more romantically, with a lantern.

When we arrived on the incoming trip, the walk to our destination was only a short distance over an avenue of soft and dazzlingly white sand that felt good between my toes when I was allowed to go barefooted. The house itself loomed in its own whiteness, with more stolidity than handsomeness, behind two large magnolia trees, like those at our house, and above a garden planted with clumps of yaupon, yucca, tea olive, daylillies, spear grass, and roses set in cleanly swept sand in which no lawn grass would grow. Like the typical South Carolina low-country houses it sat high off the ground, an impressive story-and-a-half with a wide porch running across the entire front and three large dormers fitted with green louvered shutters and decorated with scroll-saw work. A severely neat white picket fence surrounded the place, just as ours was surrounded in town.

The formality of the exterior was hardly in keeping with the casualness and provinciality of the interior. Everything inside struck me as being old-fashioned and curious. The parlor had sofas with rolls and scrolls on them. The rugs were full of faded flowers. There were enlarged family photographs on the walls, and one on an easel—draped. The chairs and the piano had fringed covers on them. The sofas had embroidered cushions and antimacassars. The curtains were lace. Vases on tables and mantels contained spear grass, cattails, peacock feathers and some plant that produced things looking like white feather dusters. And everything smelled musty.

On one of the parlor tables was a stereoscope with stunning views of Niagara Falls and the great Columbian Exposition held in Chicago in 1893, to which some member of the family (I don't know who) must have gone. These views, I must admit, I enjoyed very much.

The vast center hall, helter-skelter with miscellaneous chairs and tables, was the most cheerful spot in the house when the double doors at both ends were open and light and air swept through. And the hall seemed to extend out in the back to a long, covered porch that was the only connection of the house with the dining room and kitchen wing, otherwise a separate entity.

The double photograph of my grandparents, in a small gold frame with black edging, that my mother had on the wall in her bedroom showed the two as dignified and intelligent-looking folk. My grandfather, fully bearded and with a full head of hair, even looked distinguished in the manner of Tennyson or Longfellow, or maybe one of the Smith Brothers on the cough-drop box. My grandmother was very presentable, too, in the standard black silk dress and lace collar, with her hair drawn back and parted in the middle. Alas, old age was not becoming to her. It had made her into a shapeless blob of flesh covered with a black and white figured gingham dress and topped with a little head with swollen cheeks and a lower lip that protruded. Poor thing, she mumbled rather than talked, she was a wet kisser, and she smelled mustier than the parlor. I am afraid that I was not kind to her, for I always got away from her grasp as quickly as I could.

Aunt Stella, the oldest living daughter, was also too fleshy. Pleasant, gentle, and quiet, she always seemed to be in a gray dress of some unidentifiable material and without much shape. Aunt Hettie, with dark skin and very large eyes, was slender and reasonably tall. She was ramrod straight in her posture; and she was inclined to be frilly in her clothing. She talked in a halting, high-pitched voice, giving her conversation the impression of being artificial and unreal—like that of Dickens's Alfred Jingle. Her contacts with Bayesville were more frequent than those of my grandmother and Aunt Stella, both of whom rarely left the house except to go across the road to the house of Aunt Flora, who had married a native of Illinois named Mr. Crawford and had produced a fairly large family. Aunt Flora was small and looked remarkably like my mother. Mr. Crawford was a big, friendly, sandy-haired man.

Aunt Hettie came to town to the Baptist church in the carriage with the Crawfords, who went to the Methodist church; and she came shopping in her own buggy when she could get one of the Crawfords or a tenant to drive her. She read the *Advocate* from cover to cover and she could recite almost everything in it by heart. She was particularly interested in local society. "I see that Mrs. Mordecai Jones has had her sister, Mrs. Preston Green, visiting her from Charlotte," she would say to my mother. Or "Young Miranda Davis—has announced her engagement to some man named—Cornfield from down near Branchville. I've never heard of—the Cornfields." Or (with some disapproval) "I see that your—niece, Mrs. Wesson, has had another of her large—card parties. Twelve—tables, whatever that means. With a delicious—ice course for refreshments." My mother would only nod her head politely. She rarely read the social notes in the *Advocate,* and she hadn't the slightest interest in anybody Aunt Hettie had mentioned, except maybe Anna Maude Wesson. And she wasn't impressed by her social life either.

The other members of the family living at home and matching the spinster sisters were two bachelor brothers: Uncle Chesley, the youngest member of the family, and Uncle Harry, the oldest and the physician in the footsteps of my grandfather. Uncle Chesley looked like a big, thin rag doll and he walked like a duck. He talked in a kind of throaty gurgle around the stem of a clay pipe that he always seemed to have clenched in his stained teeth. My cousin William who managed the office of the cotton seed mill and fertilizer plant in town would frequently remark, "I saw Chesley Keller in the office today. He's the funniest man on two feet." Indeed, he was; but he was also one of the kindest and best. And he was eventually able to marry an intelligent, capable, and reasonably pretty woman who taught in the Bayesville school—a marriage that was, needless to say, a surprise to practically everybody but Uncle Chesley. He ran the farm—as much as it was run. I'm afraid that he was not the most efficient person in the world. I should also say for the record that Aunt Hettie eventually married, too, equally to our surprise. She picked out a well-to-do old widower named Mr. Bauer who built her a comfortable house on her own land adjoining Baxter and who remained around long enough to allow her to achieve some semblance of marital happiness.

Dr. Harry was a little round man with thick black hair, beetling brows, and a fuzzy black mustache. Whatever the season he was always dressed in coat and vest with a heavy gold watch chain strung across his chest and a fountain pen and thermometer peeping out of his pocket. He always frightened me to death. Once he got me in his grip, he would toss me, roll me, maul me—all in what he considered to be good-natured bearish fun but what I felt to be downright unpleasantness. What was worse, he was always giving my mother pills for me, to cure present diseases (if any) or those that I might have some remote possibility of catching in the foreseeable future. I held him responsible for the sulphur and molasses that I gagged on in the spring, or the "course" of calomel: a little wintergreen-flavored tablet that I took every day for a week. (I could never afterward tolerate the taste or smell of wintergreen.) What a frightful man he was! I fled when I caught a glimpse of him. Only on one occasion did I have any appreciation of him. That was one day when I went with him trembling in apprehension into the little white building just outside the picket fence that was his office and pharmacy. Wonder of wonders, instead of being forcibly dosed, I was courteously presented with a bag of rock candy—from the supply, I am sure, that he used to make cough syrup.

My opinion of Uncle Harry was, I am glad to report, not generally held in the community, where he was known and revered for his good works as my grandfather was. He never got rich in his profession, for he had more charity patients than he had paying ones.

Unlike Chesley and Hettie he went to his grave stalwartly unmarried.

Since my mother never liked to talk about the past or family history, I never knew very much about the Kellers, the Lehmans, Hillers, and all the other German families that were in her background. Most of them had come from the Palatinate in the eighteenth-century well before the Revolution and had settled in various places in the Orangeburgh District, some in equally appropriately named Saxe-Gotha. They were largely simple, proud people, mostly given to the soil—though among the farmers there had always been a considerable contingent of physicians. Most of them were Lutherans and some of them remained for years at least partially bilingual. My mother herself could sing a few songs in German that she had learned from one of her grandmothers. Why my physician-grandfather chose to be a Baptist, I do not know; but he went so enthusiastically into the adopted religion that he was licensed to preach. And if I may believe his obituary in one of the Columbia papers and the account in the 1902 Advocate, he was as learned as he was pious, and he was in every sense a pillar of the community. Since I never knew him, I cannot corroborate any of this from my own observation.

Although my mother revered and loved her father greatly, I believe that she did not relish thinking of some of the repressive aspects of his religion. She several times admitted that Sundays at Baxter in her girlhood could be stifling, when almost nothing was allowed except Bible-reading, prayer, and meditation. All housework came to a full stop. No food was prepared in the kitchen. Everything had to be cooked on Saturday, and the family ate picnic-style when they came back exhausted from long morning preaching services. The piano could not be opened even for religious songs, and no implement or tool—scissors, for instance—could be employed for any purpose. No needle could be used to sew on a button or mend a pair of hose. Printed matter that was not strictly religious could not be in evidence. If an ox fell into a ditch, I assume he could be pulled out; for that act had scriptual justification. Most of the other things did not. No very liberal interpretation was given to another pronouncement of our Savior to the effect that the Sabbath was made for man, not man for the Sabbath. I am afraid that, just or unjust, this kind of impression of my grandfather's strictness made me have little regret that he was not still around. Miss Millie Barton on our street was enough, and she had no parental or grandparental authority. How much worse I might fare if the old gentleman were still in the flesh. I was every inch a Barclay and not at all a Keller. No Barclay that I knew had any real trace of the pietistic in him.

My mother, too, seemed to feel more comfortable among the Barclays, for she stubbornly resisted any show of extreme piety or religious emotionalism. Her idea was that a church service should be a dignified and reverent affair, where one stood for praise, sat for instruction, and bowed for prayer. (Not kneeled as the Episcopalians had it.) Beyond these, all movements else were supererogatory. At times in place of my father who felt that Sunday evenings were made for staying at home, I accompanied my mother to evening services of the revivals that were periodically held at our church. All too often in the midst of a sermon in which the preacher had worked up a proper frenzy, thumping the pulpit and gasping in his delivery, he would take time-out for "propositions." "All those who are washed in the Blood and Saved, stand up!" he would say, while in the background the choir came in with "Whiter Than the Snow." And there would be a great rising movement among the congregation. Not my mother. She would remain sitting serene and erect. And I with her. "All those who want to go to heaven, raise the right hand." My mother's hands remained folded in her lap, and so did mine. Whereas she did not feel that a sincere conviction of Salvation was presumptuous, she regarded a public flaunting of the feeling something less than proof of the fact. Many are called, but few are chosen; and she was not going to settle for mass assertions of what might in no wise be the truth.

So in spite of the fact that Grandfather Keller was long dead, I felt that his ghost still hovered about Baxter. If the atmosphere was no longer one of oppressiveness, the household was hardly bright and sunshiny. Everybody seemed old, and, except for Uncle Chesley, serious. So as soon as I could after my arrival and the ritual of kissing, squeezing, and mauling to which I was subjected, I said, "Please, may I go and find Wilmer." Wilmer was a year or two older than I but he was the Crawford boy nearest my age, and he and I got along famously. Released, I ran across the way to the Crawford house in a flash, hoping that I'd find Wilmer there. On a pretty summer weekday he might easily be out fishing or hunting or helping his father on the farm, and in this event I might have to spend my time playing by myself. On Sundays I could count on finding him more easily.

Wilmer was one of six Crawford children. Lettice was the oldest, a sweet girl old enough to take a motherly interest in the rest of the family. Floyd, who had a slight lisp, was quiet and serious. Lura was the prettiest—a vivid brunette—and one of the brightest. Bernice was a bashful kind of blonde who seemed not to have all her wits about her. Oliver, the youngest boy, definitely did not. He was what my mother explained as "afflicted." Since he frightened me with his mutterings, I uncharitably stayed away from him as far as I could.

But Wilmer was great. He was the pick of all the people at the Keller hamlet. Black-eyed and handsome, he was a great woodsman and amateur naturalist, and he had a room full of most fascinating things: guns in racks, collections of insects and butterflies on pins, and other collections of rocks, leaves, and skins of both animals and snakes. Furthermore, he made splendid things with his hands, carving puppets, animals, windmills, and sling shots out of soft wood and making elaborate constructions of metal.

Usually he had something to give me of his own making like, for example, a chinaberry shooter that was a real prize. He made it by hollowing a straight piece of tree branch that was pithy at the center. He then whittled a ramrod to fit it. When a green chinaberry was put in the opening and the ramrod thrust forward, out flew the berry with a pop and plenty of speed. My mother disapproved of this toy, mainly because she thought that chinaberry trees—with the sickeningly sweet perfume of their delicate purplish-blue flowers in the spring and their sticky, foul-smelling berries in the summer and fall—were found only in the yards of untidy or low-caste people. She also did not relish the idea of having sticky berries brought into the house as ammunition for the gun. She could find fewer objections to the sling-shot that Wilmer made for me.

As I grew a little older and my desultory friendship with Wilmer grew, he would take me out into the woods with him to show me his rabbit traps, to identify native plants and shrubs, to go hunting for such edible wild things as huckleberries and haws, to let me shoot his twenty-two rifle (my mother was not to be told), or to go to the barnyard to see the horses and the other stock, or to go on a hot Sunday afternoon down to the creek for a bit of skinny dipping (entirely sub rosa). Sometimes we sat on logs and had man-to-man talks (though I was really the listener and had little to give back), including some illuminating things about sex. On this subject I felt that he would talk with great poise and authority and in a way that was far less slimy and dirty than that of some little boys less gentlemanly than John Morrell or Fred Collins who volunteered their misinformation. By the time he was fourteen, Wilmer was adequately initiated sexually; and, though he never openly boasted of being a Lothario or Don Juan, I was convinced that he could easily get out a comprehensive directory of all the teenaged girls in the surrounding countryside who might not decline his invitation to a tumble in the hay or the pine straw.

Wilmer, in short, was the only person at Baxter who represented life and the future to me. All the rest represented the past and death. Perhaps not paradoxically, the big events that were most fun at Baxter were the funerals. The setting was ever present. There was a handsome burial ground not far from the house, surrounded by a decorated iron fence, planted with trees and shrubs, dotted with tombstones, and spacious enough not only to accommodate those now living at the hamlet but relatives in other parts of the state who, with whatever justification, expected to find a last resting place there. The reason that funerals were fun was that family connections came from everywhere. There were always all sorts of cousins of various removes whom I had never seen before, all dressed up in their best, and bringing covered baskets of fried chicken, sliced ham, potato salad, and, one of my favorites, sweet potato pie. Tables were set up under the trees and on the large, cool front porch, and there was always plenty of iced tea and lemonade. Members of the family seemed to be most considerate when they died in the summertime (as most of them agreeably did) because outdoor picnics were then most appropriate.

So funeral days became the one kind of "entertainment" at Baxter to which I never offered any resistance. When my mother announced that Aunt So-and-So at Swansea or Cousin So-in-So at Pelion (or wherever), or even one of the Kellers of the home place had died (as at least two of them did during my childhood), I invented no reason for not going to Baxter. Rather, I was up early, scrubbed and ready to climb up the little iron steps to the coach on the Midlin. In spite of the fact that Baxter might be lugubrious enough on ordinary occasions, I was confident that the crowds of people that turned up for funerals and the numerous new children that I could find to play with would inevitably create a carnival atmosphere. And thanks to the civilized good sense of my mother and other members of the family, I was never taken in the parlor where the coffin was to "view the remains"—and incidentally to breathe the faint odor of decaying flesh beneath the sickening perfume of flowers that was so frequent a concomitant of summer funerals in the country. (My mother's disapproval of the barbaric practice of the open coffin at funerals was strong almost to the point of violence.) As a matter of fact, during the service, which could be long, the children were always encouraged to run off and play; and we consequently got as far away as possible from the goings-on until there were signs that food was being served.

So on funeral days I expected a good time at Baxter, with the knowledge that, in the end, both pleasantly stuffed with the funeral baked meats and agreeably tired from the activity of the occasion, the only thing we had to do was to flag down the six o'clock Midlin and go back to town.

IX

THE GRAVY IS THE BEST PART

THE man who says that his mother was or is the best cook in the world can lay claim to little originality. Many men have said it, and for various reasons—not the least of which, the modern woman may contend, being to irritate their wives. I never said that my mother was the best cook in the world; but others did, to her face and maybe even behind her back. And I think that, in spite of her pretense to modesty and to dislike of flattery, she rather believed it.

This is not to say that her world was large. On the contrary, it was all but limited to our small Southern town. Yet the tentacles of it could at times reach out to unexpected distances. In relatively far-away places, I have been served what hostesses have described as "your mother's" water-melon rind pickles, finger rolls, chicken salad, tomato aspic, fruit cake, or even meat loaf. These may seem to be entirely commonplace items, hardly to be found in any self-respecting gourmet's blue book. But all of them, made from long-treasured recipes, could emerge as very special in their own class and "famous" in surprising places.

My mother flourished long before Julia Child and cuisine a la television; and the *rubán bleu* or three stars in the *Guide Michelin* would have had no meaning for her. She came, as I have already explained, from a long line of German farmers, and her forebears from the Palatinate set foot in Virginia, and slightly later in South Carolina, well before the end of the eighteenth century. From her background, my mother inherited, along with her skill in cooking, a kind of cleanliness that was next door to being obsessive. Dirt was her enemy, and no speck of it was allowed to remain long within her hypersensitive view. Her kitchen, over which she presided as tutelary deity and priestess, was shining and spotless.

This, one must remember, was in a day when cleanliness was not so easy to achieve as it now is in an age of gas and electricity. The altar of my mother's temple was an iron wood stove with a cavernous oven and a capacious warming closet. Wisps of smoke sometimes escaped when the stove lids were not tight and the wind blew down the chimney; and the woodbox, which had to be constantly filled, offered some challenge to tidiness. But everything was kept shining at whatever cost, stove top as well as pots and pans.

Only on special occasions was our kitchen shared with a servant, and it was most rarely or never turned over exclusively to one. Though the economic level of our neighborhood was modest, servant hire was what we now regard as disgracefully cheap. Thus practically every woman resigned her kitchen all but entirely to a black servant. Not so my mother. As I have previously recorded, a washerwoman she had who came once a week, and a cleaning woman, and a yard man to clip the hedge and mow the lawn (though he was not trusted in her precious flower beds); and when there were guests a kitchen servant (often the cleaning woman doubling in brass) came to wash dishes. But a full-time cook, No!

On this subject no amount of persuasion or cajoling on the part of my father could do any good.

Though the kitchen may have been as clean as a laboratory, to regard it as such would be completely to miss the point. By no means was there in our kitchen the outlay of instruments and machines that now seem necessary for any kind of cooking not derived from the frozen food departments of the supermarket or from packages in which everything is powdered and dried. I do not remember seeing my mother make much to-do about measuring quantities carefully, except perhaps the liquid to be added to a package of Knox gelatine. Either as a creative cook she held herself above such routine procedures or as a confident one she deemed it unnecessary.

Yet, paradoxically, her great talent seemed to be that of being able to dictate from memory exact measurements included in a variety of elaborate recipes. This she frequently did on her front piazza where she held court on summer afternoons or over the telephone with the crank-up box in the back hall at any season of the year. I sometimes felt that half the town considered it easier to call our house than to look up something in a cook book and that my mother was operating a kind of prelapsarian dial-a-recipe service for no gain. But she did not share my attitude. Contemptuous though she was of most modern contraptions like the telephone and especially disdainful of women who used it for idle chatter, she assumed that what her "public" wanted were immediate and business-like prescriptions given with the confidence of a real professional who guaranteed success. No mere words on a printed page could, in her opinion, do the same; and she performed accordingly.

I should always say "receipt" and not "recipe." The latter was in my mother's regard a neologism hardly acceptable socially. Other verbal taboos she also had, but they were less interesting than some of her notions about food. It is not surprising that several of these should involve that most symbolic of all foods: bread. In my mother's eye no virtuous hostess (morality and food customs somehow got inextricably mixed up) would think of allowing cold bread to come to the table for any sort of formal meal. Only people of dubious status bought bakery bread at the grocery store. "Light bread" baked in our own oven and leavened with our own yeast (the produce of Fleischman was admitted late) could be used for breakfast toast or for cucumber, tomato, and pimento sandwiches to be taken to picnics or served with iced tea on summer afternoons; and beaten biscuits were a special cold bread for ladies' parties. But bread for the regular table had to be hot from the kitchen: Parker House and finger rolls light as feathers and delicately infused with the same fresh butter that helped produce their wonderful brown crust, or golden corn muffins, or biscuits so short that they would melt when they touched the lips and so small as hardly to make a discernible bite.

Nothing could be more crude than a large soda biscuit. I had this notion so firmly imbedded in my consciousness that I could only recoil in horror when, during "big recess" in grammar school, children from the cotton mill village or from the rural fringes of town pulled out such biscuits, stuffed with fried-out fat-back, from their little tin pails. Again paradoxically perhaps, of this behavior my mother did not approve. Confronted with an actual social situation, she was as far as possible from being a snob, and she would much have preferred my feeling compassion for or a desire to share with those people who were less fortunate than I, with my fresh brown paper sack neatly packed with small chicken salad sandwiches, devilled eggs, cheese biscuits, and a piece of fresh fruit according to the season—each item wrapped separately in waxed paper.

Next to bread was rice, which appeared at our noonday dinner table on every day of the world and that had a mystique and a morality all its own. Here the preparation had all the solemnity and ritual of a religious ceremony. First, came the cleansing bath in cold water with a great many changes of the water and a great deal of rubbing with the hands to assure that no surface starch remained. Then came the boiling. Next the rice was poured, amid clouds of steam, into a collander and cold water was run over it. (It took me a long time to understand the reason for this.) Back over steaming water, the rice in the collander now went to remain until it arrived on the table snowy white with each grain proudly preserving its tiny identity. Such was the triumph! If by chance two grains had stuck together, I am not entirely sure what would have happened. Such a breach of morality was unthinkable. But had it occurred, I could guess that the whole bowl would have been whisked away to exile in the pantry. In our house it was most certainly not wasted. (My mother had a proverb that she liked to quote as having come from one of her grandmothers and that ran something like: Willful waste makes woeful want.) The rice might very well have turned up the next day miraculously transformed into a sumptuous pudding, having been mixed with rich cream and eggs, butter, sugar, nutmeg, lemon rind and raisins—one of the real triumphs of my mother's cuisine.

The elaborate display of condiments and herbs usually associated with a gourmet's kitchen could not be found in that of my mother, who achieved her special flavors and aromas with what seemed to be remarkably limited means. There were the usual kinds of things like black, white, and red pepper, dry mustard, all-spice, nutmeg, cinnamon, cloves, tumeric (for pickles), and so on. Vanilla and almond extracts were always on hand for cakes and desserts, though they were supposed to be used sparingly. Whereas I remember hearing of basil, thyme, and dill, the only herbs that had any special uses were bay leaves and sage, and they not often. Sage in dried form was chiefly used for sausage and liver pudding, or stuffing for fowl; green sage from a generous low-growing bush in our garden sometimes was brewed into a charmingly aromatic and pungent tea that I was given when my stomach was queasy. Mint from a variety of plants regularly was used for jelly and as decoration for iced tea glasses. Onions we had and they were often used for seasoning. But I never saw a garlic clove until I was quite grown. Monosodium glutamate would have inspired little more than incredulity in our house.

As every Southerner knows, vegetables required, other than salt and pepper, only two kinds of seasoning: that of ham hock and the kind of bacon called streak of fat and streak of lean—both of which elicited from string beans or peas a "potlikker" fit for the gods when poured over golden, crumbly cornbread. People from other areas of the country have often been derogatory of Southern vegetable dishes which they have found to be overcooked and swimming in grease. The modern style of steaming vegetables was virtually unknown in my mother's kitchen, string beans in particular being allowed to simmer half a day in an iron pot on the back of the Charter Oak range. Yet excessive grease in any vegetable dish would have been regarded as decidedly low caste and not to be tolerated. Cabbage was never allowed to become a greasy, foul-smelling mush and was not infrequently served crisp from brief boiling with light seasoning of pepper and salt and a slight glaze of butter. A combination of yellow squash and chopped onions cooked with a little butter or bacon fat could be a memorable dish. Another one that might seem sacrilegious to a palate accustomed to the best of fresh tossed salads was wilted lettuce, delicately achieved, with bits of crisp breakfast bacon.

Spinach was virtually unknown in our vegetable repertory, but why should one worry about such tasteless stuff when one had the full-bodied and tangy flavor of properly cooked mustard or turnip greens or the tantalizingly odoriferous and delicately sweet collards? This last vegetable left on the stalk until after the first frost, cooked so as to be only slightly glazed with bacon fat, and served with a succulent, golden baked sweet potato and corn pone has been an enduring delight to the true Southern palate, plebeian and aristocratic tastes coinciding in enthusiastic approval.

It is hardly necessary to say a great deal about the cooking of fowl, beef, and pork, most of which followed traditional patterns. The fried chicken at our house might have been only slightly better than that of Colonel Sanders at his best, but the superb thing about it was the milk gravy that metamorphosed rice and hominy grits into minor divinities. In this connection, the most elegant breakfast among my mother's menus had as its staples fried chicken with milk gravy, hominy grits (of necessity), and waffles. A steak breakfast was a special occasion: country fried steak also, with delicious gravy achieved partly from the flour beaten into the steak. More commonplace, but equally appealing, was a breakfast of fried country ham with red-eye gravy, designed to fill an entrancing little well in a fluffy white mound of hominy grits, long and expertly cooked. In fact, the gravies—always gravies never sauces—at our house were always so good that I once chose "The Gravy Is the Best Part" for a cook book that never progressed beyond the title.

Rare roast beef and rare steak I never experienced

until I left home. Roast beef and roast pork were alike well done—the one to a rich moist brownness and the other to a delicate and white dryness. Meat loaf made of finely ground beef and pork, bread crumbs, fresh tomatoes, chopped onions, and green peppers, topped with bacon strips and a little brown sugar, could be good enough for a banquet. Hams were traditionally well basted with their own juices, glazed with brown sugar, and porcupined with cloves. Baked turkey and chicken were stuffed, as one would expect, with oysters, chestnuts, and bread crumbs, though one of our specialties was a different kind of dressing made of the turkey or chicken stock, flour, cornmeal, eggs, and condiments and cooked in a baking pan so that it could be scored in succulent squares for easy serving.

For festive or formal meals there was rarely just a single salad. And here I should say that tossed salads as we now know them were rare at our table, though one might on ordinary occasions have lettuce along with thinly sliced cucumbers, tomatoes, and radishes topped with home-made mayonnaise or with a special cooked dressing made with eggs, dry mustard, flour, and vinegar somewhat in the same manner in which Hollandaise sauce is made. This, however, was not what the word salad meant most often to my mother. The regular trio for a full-dress dinner included potato salad, fresh fruit salad made of oranges, white grapes, and melon, and a great chicken salad to which a finely chopped apple lent a special flavor in combination with the regular celery, boiled eggs, and so on. Congealed fruit and vegetable salads and aspics were admissible chiefly for luncheons; and frozen salads were virtually unknown except for ladies' bridge parties for which, in the absence of refrigerators with freezing units, they had to be made clumsily in a regular ice-cream freezer (with dasher removed) kept on the back porch.

Ice cream, of course, was a great summer staple, especially in the peach season when the crank of the back-porch freezer seemed to be daily in operation. Other fruits in season were used, too. But nothing was so impressive as the peach ice cream, made with a boiled custard into which great bowls of rich and wonderful whipped cream had been folded. In my mother's world few people seemed to worry about cholesterol.

Various seasons for fruits and vegetables provided during the summer months what seemed to be a continuous process of pickling, preserving, and canning that stocked our pantry shelves with a tantalizing array of glass jars, appealing aesthetically, because of their varicolored contents, as well as gastronomically.

Wine was also a part, albeit limited, of my mother's repertory. The basic one seems to have been blackberry wine, a full-bodied, sweet liquid with a good deal of authority. This refreshment was always served in the parlor with a piece of fruit cake, usually black fruit cake, to afternoon female callers until hot weather forced the serving of iced tea and little sandwiches on the piazza. (Hot tea in the afternoon was never a custom with us.) The wine was also used to season a wide variety of desserts involving whipped cream: for example, tipsy cake, floating island, charlotte russe, and a standard Christmas delicacy called syllabub, sometimes served as an alternate to another standard holiday dessert, ambrosia.

Scuppernong wine seemed to be the hardest to achieve. When it was successful, it had the light gold color and the exquisite flavor of the fresh grape nurtured in a warm southern sun. When it failed, as it seemed to do on numerous occasions, it served as a useful and tasty wine vinegar. There was a peach wine, too, though I remember it as being a little too sweet for my palate. The most unusual wine was made of tomatoes. It looked and tasted like a light rosé. I never knew how any of these wines were made. I merely knew that the process took place in the summertime and that the bottles were stored in a dark, aromatic closet along with brandied peaches and cherries, delicacies that saw the light only during high feasts like Thanksgiving and Christmas.

Cakes, pies, what an array of them came out at these seasons! Christmas, for example, was never complete without a battery of cakes, including white and dark fruitcakes, a coconut cake, a chocolate layer cake, and a Lady Baltimore cake. Mincemeat, apple, and cherry pies, not to mention the supreme pecan and coconut cream pies, were also at times somehow fitted into the staggering menus when twenty or more members of the family trooped in for the kind of meal that they could annually expect at more than half a dozen places. Anyone who has ever been subjected to the agony of having to turn up for a midday and an evening family dinner at different places on the same day during the Thanksgiving or Christmas season might wonder how anybody ever survived or, if he did, how he could look back fondly on the food that was served. But, as everyone knows, excessively lavish feasts have been perpetrated since the beginning of recorded time; and ours in the light of history were not extraordinary. In the high seasons my mother knew that she could queen it over her sisters and sisters-in-law and, though she ordinarily was a thrifty person, she spared no expense or labor at these times to establish her hegemony.

Food in the world that I have been talking about, as it should now be obvious, was the province and prerogative of women. I knew that chefs presided over kitchens in fashionable restaurants and in large hotels. (I even had some remote notion of Escoffier of the Ritz.) I also knew that men in greasy aprons turned out greasy food in short-order places and that certain men servants in bachelor establishments had been trained to broil steaks and chops. Yet I was almost grown before it occurred to me that a man who made any pretense to masculinity or social acceptability ever ventured into a kitchen to cook. Outdoor cooking such as I was instructed to do in my Boy Scout troop or such as grown men did on hunting and fishing trips (though here black male servants were usually taken along) might have been admissible. My own father, who was handy in many other domestic areas, did not know the first principles of cooking; and, though I might have been tempted by tantalizing smells and the possibility of delicious tidbits to enter, I was most often very firmly encouraged to stay out of the kitchen, being allowed to lick a cake bowl or the dasher from an ice-cream churn only if I remained on the back porch. When years later as a bachelor I built a small house of my own, my mother viewed with grave concern the fact that I insisted upon a well-equipped kitchen. Of what use could it possibly be unless I did what she had never done—that is, employed a male servant? Eating out was a far more gentlemanly and practical thing to do until I found it feasible to change my status and establish a real home, when presumably my wife would take over the kitchen. Anything that I attempted to do would be, if not vulgar, at least farcical.

Cooking was a mission, a cult, an art. It had aspects of drudgery, too. But the element of creativity that it offered provided the kind of liberation that any artist feels in objectifying his ideas. And for my mother it produced evidence of a superiority that placed womanhood in more than favorable competition with the crass male world. It is only in a time when women en masse have invaded the materialistic world of business

X

WAR AND GAMES

O N June 28, 1914, sixteen days after my eighth birthday, Archduke Francis Ferdinand of Austria was assassinated by Gavrolo Princep at Sarajevo. I had little idea of what the affair meant; but since in my stamp collection were two or three large and beautiful stamps of Bosnia-Hercegovina, I had some general notion of the geography involved. It was, however, wonderful summertime; and I was too busy playing in a neighborhood generously endowed with children to be very much aware either of the initial event or of the tragic crescendo of happenings in the remote distance that led to "the baleful and tragic guns of August."

The year after the war in Europe got under way, the Badhams moved into the green house across from me; and Damon, the younger of the two sons, decided that he would organize an "army" so that we could have a war of our own in Plum Tree Lane simulating the one going on across the ocean. Before Fred Collins left the green house, we had encountered *Tarzan of the Apes*, which was almost so fresh from the press that the ink had not fully dried. Under its spell we had begun engaging in such primitive sports as swinging from trees and stalking imaginary wild animals. Since Damon was about two years older than Fred and I, he was far more sophisticated about what was going on in the world. Besides, in 1915 Robert L. Drake (né C.W. Hayes) had begun bringing out a series of boys' books about World War I with a new one about every three or four months; and Damon introduced us to such examples of them as *The Boy Allies in the Trenches* and *The Boy Allies on the North Sea Patrol,* or *Striking the First Blow at the German Navies.* So Tom Swift and Tarzan had to take a back seat for the moment. Damon had something of the Prussian in him, even if his sympathies were ultimately to be on the other side; thus one day he announced curtly that he was organizing an army of which he would be Commander in Chief and Generalissimo (though the latter word may not have been in his vocabulary at the time) and that I was to be Adjutant General. I had no idea what my proposed title meant. It was, no matter, an offer that I could not refuse. The truth is that I was overawed and even hypnotized by Damon's intensity, expressed in his steely eyes and hard gaze. So I went along, not smart enough to discover for some time that I was to be chiefly his batman or orderly.

The "army" was less than minuscule. We could count as our "troops" only Fred Collins, two Hamilton boys from across the railroad tracks, and ourselves. And even Fred and the Hamilton boys were not around all the time. Thus most of the army had to be pieced out through imagination, of which Damon had more than an adequate supply. Though he was quite precocious in every way, I don't think he had read Shakespeare's prologue to *Henry V,* but nothing could have expressed his theory better:

> And let us ciphers in this great accompt,
> On your imaginary forces work
> . . . .
> Piece out our imperfections with your thoughts;
> Into a thousand parts divide one man,
> And make imaginary puissance.

Damon made imaginary puissance like crazy, compiling a large muster roll from telephone directories, indexes of books, and out of his own fertile brain—to be stashed in a place so secret that even I did not know its whereabouts.

John Morrell had moved across town and was now living in "enemy" territory. But he was not an enemy himself. I saw to that. Bigger boys like Dewey Collins and Roderick Badham were potential enemies, but they belonged to no identifiable army. In fact, the enemy army was vague in the extreme. About the only thing agreed upon about it was that it existed and that it was lurking, well entrenched, in the northern section of town, always threatening to march through Plum Tree Lane as the German army had marched (according to *The Boy Allies at Liege*) through Belgium.

So we must begin our own program of "Preparedness"—build forts, gather ammunition, dig trenches, and train our "troops." Forts we did begin building at breakneck speed. First, we "fortified" the Badham woodhouse, constructing a lookout on top, stocking it with a pile of throwable and shootable (in slingshots) rocks, and all the B-B shot that we could afford to buy at the hardware store down town. Then we built a fort in a chinaberry tree in a lower Badham garden. Next we dug trenches in the pasture close to the creek as a first line of defense, and connected the trench with a dugout that we had to enter by crawling.

Even though we had heard that President Wilson was asking everybody to be strictly neutral and that he was determined to keep us out of the European war, our "enemy," thanks to the effective propaganda of Robert L. Drake and his "Boy Allies," could hardly have been other than the Germans. But under the influence of the "Katzenjammer Kids" in the funnies we still regarded them somewhat comically; and we had not yet been taught to hate them as we later were. So they were simply "enemies" in the same sense that the Indians had earlier been in our games.

What I did not know about warfare, Damon with some condescension set out to teach me. One of the first things he told me I must learn was that all military communications had to be by secret code, known only to those who had code books. Sometimes people memorized the books and then burned them, or in extreme cases even swallowed them. Damon had already invented a code—which I decided later he had either plagiarized or adapted from Poe's *The Gold Bug*. I was given a copy of it. I didn't have to memorize and burn or swallow it, but it was to be kept in a very secret place. I decided it should be under a removable bottom of an old elaborately carved armoire or wardrobe in the guest bedroom. Another copy was hidden in a tin can buried under the coal pile in the fort.

On a given morning Damon might appear at our front door before breakfast looking mysterious. (He was not now a general but a messenger or spy.) Without saying a word, he would take a piece of paper out of his shirt and pass it to me, indicating by gesture that I should conceal it on my person as quickly as possible. Out from the wardrobe floor would come my copy of the code—of course, when nobody was looking—and I would slowly decipher: "Report to hedqtrs imediatly the enemy plans to attact at 2 p.m. today." After breakfast I would run over to join the general in his headquarters (a corner of his bedroom); and, maintaining all the mystery of the delivery of the dispatch, he would lead me out of the house to begin the operations of the day: that is, the strengthening of the forts and the stockpiling of more ammunition. Spies, Damon would confide, had advised him of a troop build-up just north of us and an army led by Angus McCarson, a dark-haired, flat-nosed local bully whom I knew too well from his attempts to waylay me and whose transformation into a "German" I was thus perfectly willing to accept.

On a day when spies warned us that there would be an "attact" at two p.m., Damon and I could be found in the fort busily peering through spy-glasses (cardboard mailing tubes that had been used for calendars), priming our air rifles, and lining up rocks for the slingshots. Strongly influenced by Damon's imagination, I was usually full of suspense, convinced that Angus, indeed, might be out there watching us with some of his cronies and readying a march on us. Of course, nobody turned up. But one day Roderick and Dewey hove into view. They were, it is true, just walking about in the backyard, minding their own business and having no designs on the fort. Nevertheless, we were expecting the enemy and willy-nilly they were it.

I was at my post at one of the slits, air rifle in hand. The gun was cocked and I was ready. When the two boys got to a point at which I could see "the whites of their eyes," the General ordered "Fire" and I did, striking Roderick with a B-B shot somewhere in the area of his stomach. There could have been merely a sting, but Roderick gave a yelp as if he had been murdered. And both of our enemies were as mad as hatters. They shouted to us to come out and said they would "get" us even if we didn't. When we didn't emerge, they got themselves some rocks to throw and settled down to a siege. A good many rocks hit the sides of the fort with loud bangs, but we felt safe inside for we had the wooden shutters and the door securely barred, and we could fire back well enough to keep the older boys out of too close range. It was, however, dark and suffocating inside. So we heaved a sigh of relief when after two or three hours the enemy got bored and decided to go down town for "dopes" (local dialect for Coca-Colas) at the Fain Drug Store. I sneaked out of the fort and ran home as fast as I could. The next day, I spent with John Morrell, giving the Badham house wide berth.

This was not the end of our war games by any means. We kept on playing in the fort not only all that summer, but at least sporadically into the next year. On days when Fred and the Hamiltons were around, we drilled down in the pasture by the trenches and the dugout. Damon, of course, gave all the orders, snapping at us younger ones in the way that he thought military presonnel of rank ought to do. As the months went by, he grew more and more serious, withdrawn, and quarrelsome. Then one day, with no apparent reason, he turned on me in a rage, saying that I was a traitor and ordering me off the place on pain of being shot or hanged if I set foot in the yard again.

I left as I was ordered and for a long time I did not go back. When I encountered Damon at school, he merely tightened his lips and stared stonily in the opposite direction. I noticed that he had become progressively paler and that his face seemed to be swollen. Then he was sent away to a hospital in Columbia for a long time. When he came back, he had to stay in bed.

I was curious enough to ask my father one day what kind of disease Damon had. "A leaking heart," he said, "but he is not to know it. So you mustn't discuss it with your friends." "A leaking heart," I thought, and my mind conjured up a chilling image associated with a framed chromo of the bleeding heart of Jesus that I had seen at the Trigmans'. I couldn't get the picture out of my mind.

One day my mother made boiled custard and I took a tray over with custard, cake, a comic book, and some flowers on it. I went with a good deal of hesitancy, for I did not know what to say and I feared that Damon's irrational hatred might flare up again. It did not. When I entered the room, he held out his frail hand, and we were immediately good friends once more. I went over several times after that for brief visits. But in a month or so he was dead.

It was the first death of a contemporary that I had experienced. It should have shocked me. But somehow it did not, for everything about it was completely unreal. Damon was taken to a family burial ground down state that was too far away for me to go to the funeral. Afterward my mother let me go over to take a bouquet of cut flowers for the house. Mrs. Badham with tears in her eyes kissed me on the forehead. "Damon has left us," she said. That was all. It occurred to me that his coffin should have had a flag covering it and some guns should have been fired, as he had once explained to me was fitting for the burial of soldiers. But I didn't ask. I couldn't, for his mother would not have understood. So the first "casualty" in the war in Plum Tree Lane passed into history.

The war in Europe, by this time, had seemed to come to a standstill with the Germans stopped short of Paris. Most of the fighting was at sea, and there was suspenseful news about how the German battleship *Blücher* was sunk by the British. Then came the sinking of the *Lusitania* off the coast of Ireland, with the loss of a thousand people, more than two hundred of whom were Americans. The *Literary Digest* carried pictures that made an impression on me, especially one of Alfred G. Vanderbilt whose last words to his valet before he went down with the ship were reported as something like "Find the kiddies." In short, women and children like me had been drowned—many of both. The horror was not lost on me; and whatever image I may have had of the Germans beforehand, I began to feel that their policy of "frightfulness" in the U-boat campaign and their threats to blockade us made them monsters.

After the *Titanic* went down, there was a cartoon showing the ship in the palm of a great white hand, most of which was submerged in the ocean. "The Hand of God" the caption commented rather obviously. For the sinking of the *Lusitania* a cartoonist had contrived a matching drawing: a huge white skull in Pickelhaube with ships sinking in the ocean all around it. The caption read: "Another Iceberg." (Having taught myself the rudiments of journalistic cartooning, I was very much taken by such things.)

Two years or more later when we were fully at war and Hollywood was cranking up its machinery to turn out propaganda films like *War Brides* with Alla Nazimova and *The Little American* with Mary Pickford, I went on a business trip with my father to Columbia; and in the afternoon we decided to see a movie called *The Kaiser the Beast of Berlin.* It was about the sinking of the *Lusitania.* I can't remember the film in detail. But the Kaiser, played by Rupert Julian, was in every sense a beastly villain, who having ordered the destruction of the ship was eventually haunted (ostensibly in the Sans-Souci Palace at Potsdam) by the captain of the U-boat. The latter had been driven to stark insanity by the memory of what he had done. On me this kind of propaganda worked with moderate success.

Something related to war but that was more cheerful than all this kind of horror, I am glad to say, occurred in the summer of 1916 when a National Guard unit had an encampment in Bayesville for maneuvers. The regiment pitched tents at the Tri-County Fair Grounds and had wonderful parades in town, with the officers looking splendid on their horses and the men impressive on foot. They also had grown-up war games with skirmishes in wooded areas like Hunter's Wood at the end of our street; and there was much shooting of blank cartridges as medical corpsmen rushed around taking the "wounded" away on stretchers to be picked up by ambulances, some of them horse drawn. A few field pieces were wheeled out and fired, chiefly on the railroad station square, which was being "defended."

Making the event pertinent and even a bit frightening was the fact that on the preceding March 9, Pancho Villa, the Mexican revolutionary, had made a murderous raid on Columbus, New Mexico, and General Pershing had marched into Mexico to get him. I read some of the newspaper headlines about this frustrated expedition, at times shivering with fear lest the devil Villa should break out of Mexico again to "get" us. I had no accurate idea of distances, but this possibility seemed ever so much more vivid for the moment than any of the threats offered by the fighting in Europe or on the seas. So the appearance of real live soldiers in our village was not only exciting but also reassuring.

All my playmates loved the soldiers and begged their parents to invite them for meals. We had two for supper early in the week, and they remained my friends throughout the encampment, winking to me as they marched by in the parades and saving the empty shells of their cartridges for me. Warfare on the level on which they played it seemed to be a delightful adventure, and far more exciting than Damon's. But I could get far enough away from the illusion at this point to admit to myself that I should not at all like to be in a position where I might be shot at with real bullets.

Yet the romantic illusion did continue, for in a month or two we had a visit from one of the numerous emissaries from Europe who flocked to the United States at the time to drum up sympathy for the Allied cause. Our propagandist was a handsome young British lieutenant who called himself "leftenant" and who was all resplendent in shining boots, Sam Browne belt, and a jaunty cap. Little boys followed him about the streets and the young girls were mad about him. I gave out handbills for him, announcing that he would speak on "Britain and German Kultur" at the school auditorium. My reward was a splendid autographed photograph. I could not have asked for more. *The Kaiser the Beast of Berlin* and the visit of "Leftenant" Gerald Pryce-Smith had gone a long way toward my conversion to the Allied point of view.

Yet a certain amount of ambivalence remained. The Democratic slogan in 1916 for reelection of Woodrow Wilson, as it was printed in big letters under poster photographs of the President, was "HE KEPT US OUT OF THE WAR," and the natural assumption was that we were going to stay away from Europe. At the same time, the Germans were sinking more ships with Americans on them, and everybody was talking about "Preparedness." My mother, who, as the popular song was putting it, had not brought up her son to be a soldier, was worrying about what would happen to my brother James in the event of our entering the struggle; and not a little of her anxiety rubbed off on me. Suddenly much of the steam that I had worked up for rushing to the aid of Britain and France vanished. I did not want my brother to have to go to the Army, for I was convinced that once he was shipped off to France he would inevitably wind up under one of those crosses in the fields where poppies blow, just as Lieutenant-Colonel McCrae described in the poem that everybody was quoting.

When war was actually declared in 1917 and both the attendant hysteria and the Selective Service took over, all the draftable young men in the village were daily being waved off at the station on trains taking them to camps of one sort or another. And almost daily, troop trains would come through, shuttling new recruits from one cantonment to another. These were always cheered by flag-waving girls and served coffee, doughnuts, and fruit by older women in Red Cross uniforms with flowing white hoods. The ubiquitous poster by James Montgomery Flagg, showing Uncle Sam pointing a remarkably searching and commanding finger, was doing its work. Either that or the institution of the draft. Clarence Trigman from our block went into the Army, and so did Lawrence Collins a week or two later. Dewey ran away and, though underage, enlisted in the Marine Corps. Two of Aunt Clarina's sons, Whitman and Jack Connor, were drafted, the first electing the Navy and the second the Army. Mrs. Gerston's brother also went. Little service flags with one or two stars in them were, therefore, waving from doorposts or pasted in windows all along Plum Tree Lane. But there was none at our house. At this point, I must admit that my attitude was, again, ambivalent. I did not want James to go to war, but I should have liked ever so much to have one of the little flags fluttering from our doorpost. And I certainly did not want anybody to think that we had a "slacker" in the family. I was smart enough to recognize that the prejudice against men who were out of service for any reason would be very virulent indeed, though maybe not so much in Bayesville as in other areas that I read about in the papers where "yellow feathers" were pinned on people, faces were spat on, and other kinds of physical violence were employed.

My brother fortunately escaped local notice for two main reasons. First, he was fairly far away and had been so for six or seven years; and, second, he had a reasonably important job in a war industry. In fact, he was a junior executive in a war plant in Hoboken that manufactured ignition systems on Army and Navy contracts. If I remember correctly, he did not come home for the duration of the war. His absence was not due to a matter of shame, I wanted to believe, but rather to his working around the clock and around the year. At any rate, we missed the opportunity of having a handsome and gallant soldier in the family and a service flag with a blue star in it. But a live brother, I rationalized, was better than a dead hero represented by a cross and some poppies.

As far as our local experience with Germans was concerned, we had had only one in town that anybody could remember—not counting all those people like my mother's family who had been around since the seventeenth or the eighteenth century. Our German was named Herman Klask, who lived and had a photography studio over the Fain Drug Store. He was a dark, ugly little man who wore black, baggy clothes and large gold-rimmed spectacles. I remember chiefly the pervasive odor of his quarters produced by the kerosene stove on which he cooked his meals and the chemicals that he used in his trade. He was a loner like Charlie Lee, the Chinese laundryman; and with his heavy accent he had almost as little conversation as Charlie, who apparently knew only a few words of English. But though people thought that he was curious, nobody disliked him or feared him; and in a small town like ours it was only natural to be nice to strangers.

But then suddenly one day after news had come about America's breaking off diplomatic relations with Germany, Mr. Klask disappeared—into thin air. Nobody saw him go, and nobody had any idea when he had gone. He had been a spy all the time! Just what he could possibly have spied on in Bayesville is hard to say. But a spy he was or a "saboteur," one of those that had "honeycombed" the whole country. If there was little in Bayesville to spy on, there was also little to blow up—no large power transformers, no depots of raw or military materials, no factory manufacturing war goods—except maybe the Middleville Mill that made nothing more strategic than bed ticking. Had our spy-saboteur been picked up by a U-boat lurking off the coast not too far away, or could he be hiding out in the woods somewhere, waiting to do something dastardly to the community—ah, yes, like poisoning the water supply? This last idea took hold. Stories were going around in the newspapers about poisoned water systems; so the city fathers decided to put a guard on our water tank and lights were strung up the one hundred or more feet of ladder to catch little Mr. Klask as he climbed up with a can of cyanide in his hand. As for me, I was at first apprehensive, then skeptical, and finally I was delighted because the sight of the illuminated water tank reminded me of the lights on the ferris wheel at carnivals and the fair, and I thought the effect quite grand like the pictures I'd seen of the Eiffel Tower at night.

Thus the people who had attempted with all good will, and in spite of little success, to be kind and hospitable to Mr. Klask now feared and hated him. But hate was the order of the day, and there were even manuals to tell you how to do it. Take, for example, a pamphlet called "Know Your Enemy" put out by the Sons of the Revolution, picturing on the first page a heavy-jowled and scowling von Hindenburg over a large handle-bar mustache—a "Blond Beast," preparing to hiss, "I have the right to do what I have the power to do." Next there was the Kaiser, haughty and sinister, a "Godless prince," looking out "upon a world he had drenched in blood." "Hear your would-be Master's voice," the Sons of the Revolution enjoined as the pamphlet piled quotation upon quotation, example upon example to demonstrate the "barbarities of the Prussian Beast" committed not only in word but in deed. Reading through this book was guaranteed to make anybody hate enthusiastically. "Hate" posters, too, sprang up in many places. The most violent was the one that depicted the Kaiser in spiked helmet and with a mouth like a tiger's in which he was chewing up women and children—undoubtedly Belgians, the blood dripping from his lips. The Beast of Berlin, indeed!

What effect the hate campaign actually had on us must, however, have been minimal. Now that Mr. Klask was gone, we had no German to revile in person. And we should not have willingly stopped reading the "Katzenjammer Kids" on Sunday morning if the paper had not dropped the strip. Rudolph, the dastardly villain in black mustachios and an opera cape over a perpetual full-dress suit, might easily have been German; but he stayed in the funnies, always menacing the blonde Belinda who was always saved in the nick of time by the handsome "Hairbreadth Harry."

On a far higher level than "Know Your Enemy" was a pretty little book of undetermined sponsorship called *World War Hero Alphabet—Illustrated.* Its stated purpose was to make the "great war easier for school children to learn about" by giving photographs of the Allied leaders, with rhymes about them in alphabetical sequence, in order to help us identify them readily if by chance we should meet them walking down our main street. For example:

> H is for Haig,
> British Marshall of renown,
> Who with his fighting Tommies
> Helped smash the Kaiser's crown!

> P is for Pershing,
> Our Jack so brave and cheery,
> Whose Yankees won world freedom
> At Sedan and Chateau-Thierry.

or a sentimental one—

> Q is for Queen Mary,
> England's rarest flower,
> Who nursed the boys and brought them joys
> In Britain's darkest hour.

An inescapable part of our learning about the war was the Liberty Bond and patriotic rallies that seemed to be held on every available occasion. In school we were urged, in addition to helping our parents plant war gardens, to give our pennies through the Red Cross to the war victims, especially the Belgian children, and to convert into Thrift Stamps those pennies we had left. We were also enjoined to sell Thrift Stamps to our neighbors. In this endeavor I was a little more successful than I had been trying to sell postcards in order to get a pony. I supposed that patriotism was the explanation. For the elementary schools there was even a *Liberty Loan Primer* written by Porter Emerson Brown and illustrated by James Montgomery Flagg—the latter of whom seemed forever serving his country with pen or brush and palette. One preposterous sample—a "hate" one—will serve:

> This Is A Kai-ser.
> What Is A Kai-ser?
> A Kai-ser Is A Blood-thirsty
> Old An-ac-ro-nism
> All Cov-ered With Ho-kum.
> Why Should Kai-sers Still
> Live when Do-dos and Five
> Toed Hors-es Are Ex-tinct?
> Cheer up. Give us time.

I figured that a lot of time would be necessary to answer that one, and I did not see the relation it might have to a sales ploy.

Not to be outdone by poets inferior to myself who were in there pitching, I contrived a verse of my own for a bond drive which ran—

> We must work with all our might
> While our boys in Flanders fight,
> Build the ships and make the guns
> To defeat the beastly Huns.

In fact, I filled a whole notebook with things like this, illustrated with my own pen and several colors of ink as

James Montgomery Flagg had done for his books. Another verse scarcely better I quote only because it deftly squeezed in three of the most popular cliches of the time:

> We must save the world for democracy,
> Crush the forces of autocracy,
> Raise our banners to the stars
> To win the war to end all wars!

In spite of all the dreadful verse, mine and otherwise, the Liberty Bond and Red Cross rallies did fairly well in our town. The 1917 Town Directory proudly reported:

> BAYESVILLE IS PATRIOTIC—About a score of her boys have volunteered (sic) in the service of the nation, she subscribed $27,000 for the Liberty Loan Fund and $1,000 for the Red Cross.

My father bought so many Liberty Bonds that he got a medal from the Treasury Department. With the medal came some sort of red, white, and blue certificate; so we at last had something to paste in a window in lieu of a flag with a blue star.

Blue stars in some windows at times were being replaced by gold ones, and there were several gold stars in the service flag flying at the Post Office. Fortunately, none of the gold stars had to be inserted into flags on our street. We did have, nevertheless, one period of serious fright, for there was a day when a boy on a bicycle stopped at Aunt Clarina's house and pulled a yellow envelope from his cap. As usual the news spread rapidly; and in seconds my mother had got out of her apron and had run over to see what the dreadful news could be. When she got there, several neighbors had already arrived, and Aunt Clarina was sitting in her parlor pale as a ghost with the open telegram in her lap. It was from the War Department and it was about Jack. But he had not been killed. He had been gassed and was in a hospital "Somewhere in France." This was bad enough, for nobody knew what being gassed meant. So there were several weeks of anxiety before a letter from Jack himself allayed fears. It was our closest call. Now in the thought that Jack would come home a hero, we felt that Aunt Clarina should be proud indeed.

As precocious a reader as I may have pretended I was, I was not on hand at the Bayesville Public Library when the translation of Blasco Ibanez's *The Four Horsemen of the Apocalypse* was put on the "new" shelf sometime in 1918; thus I had not read the rather bulky novel. Moreover, since Miss Millie Barton had neglected to explicate Revelations VI, 1-8 in our Sunday School class, I did not know that along with Conquest, War, and Famine—all names of horses, I gathered—was a pale horse named Pestilence. I was, therefore, not aware of the association of War, which produced gold stars for heroes who died gloriously overseas; with Pestilence, which could take people off anywhere without any glory whatsoever. Some better recognition of this fact came in September of 1918.

The day was a dank, miserable, rainy one some time after the middle of the month. After school I had drifted down to my father's store on Pine Street, and I was at the front entrance leaning idly against one of the iron columns. Across the street I saw one of my several local cousins, Marian Barclay, lower her umbrella and enter Mr. Fallon's furniture store. Marian was eighteen and a high-spirited, attractive girl who was in her second year as a music major at the Greenville Female College. I liked her very much and she returned the compliment. I knew that Marian frequently dropped in at Mr. Fallon's because she liked to play on the pianos that were always on display, along with a few reed organs, at the front of the store. Besides, Mr. Fallon was always delighted to have her try out the new instruments so that he could use her opinion as a sales pitch to prospective customers. So deciding to hear Marian play, I crossed the street. When I entered the store, I discovered that instead of sitting at the Knabe baby grand that was the jewel of the collection, she had put a roll on a player piano and was pumping away. The arrangement of "A Long, Long Trail" that the piano was playing was pretty enough, but it did little to brighten the gloom of the rainy afternoon. I'd have preferred something not so good musically but more cheerful like "K-K-K-Katy." As I stood slightly behind her, Marian appeared not to observe me. But when the piece was finished and the roll was clicking in the slot, she pivoted almost as if she were an automaton and said in a flat voice, "Susan Whitfield has just died. Influenza. She was expecting." I was properly stunned. I knew that Susan had married Roy Whitfield a few months ago when he was getting ready to go to camp and that he had recently been shipped off to France. But I did not know that she was ill and certainly not that she was pregnant. (If I had known the latter fact, I could not have said the word, just as Marian felt that she couldn't.) My shock was not due at the moment entirely to the double tragedy involved but to a more immediate realization that in the event a threat to the whole town was imminent. The spectre of a dreaded epidemic was now inescapably among us. So as a reply to Marian, I gasped a sort of "Oh," added "I must tell Aunt Allie," and ran back to my father's store.

The succeeding week brought accounts of more deaths; and precautions against the disease were being taken frantically everywhere. Church services and public meetings of all sorts were cancelled. The moving picture theater was closed. The Red Cross ladies in the big room over a down-town store stopped rolling bandages and knitting sweaters for shipment overseas and started making gauze masks for protection at home. People were wearing them on the streets and wherever they had reluctantly to assemble, the idea being that germs of the pestilence doubtless put into the air by the Germans could be effectively trapped in the gauze.

Then one morning both my mother and I found ourselves with headaches and with a weakness that kept us from getting up. The epidemic had got us. My father, who could hardly boil water, surveyed the grim situation and produced something hot for us to drink—milk or tea, I've forgotten which—before he called a doctor. By this time, my physician-uncle, Dr. Harry Keller, had died, and we had a local physician named Dr. Templeman, a tall, thin, dark-complexioned man who talked laconically through his nose but was not so frightening as Uncle Harry. He came, looked at our tongues, put thermometers in our mouths, listened with a stethoscope to our chests and backs, wrote out a sheaf of prescriptions, and departed, assuring us as he did so that we had IT and that we had better be damned careful in following a regimen that he was going to write out for us. He never did, but his exit was impressive enough to make us feel that he was not joking about our disease.

I don't know how scared my mother was. As usual, she showed no fright, simulating her standard Stoic acceptance. As for me, I was all but out of my wits. I fully expected to die. I wasn't an old person or a pregnant woman, but the statistics regarding the types of people most likely to die in the epidemic were not yet available to me; and I assumed that the thing to do when one got the disease was to die. Damon had died, and I supposed that I could, too. But somehow I didn't like the idea.

No matter how uncomfortable my mother and I were, it was my father who bore the brunt of the affair. Aunt Allie could manage the store, but there was nobody to take care of us. Ginsy and Dittie did not show their faces, and other people that my father tried to get were engaged elsewhere. Our house, unlike houses in England during the seventeenth-century plague that

Defoe wrote about, did not have a securely barred front door with a cross painted on it, but it might just as well have had. Neighbors would come and leave quantities of excellent food on our front porch or they would talk to my father if he went to a window, but few would come in. So in the eerie isolation of the situation, my father had to manage as best as he could, following instructions faithfully, if clumsily; that my mother issued from her bed. A prime problem was, of course, keeping her there, for she felt that neither rain, snow, sleet, nor pestilence should prevent her from making her appointed domestic rounds.

Once or twice we had a visit from the county nurse. In her stiffly starched uniform, almost blindingly white to weak eyes, she moved with efficiency and assurance in the sick room—taking temperatures, giving sponge baths, rearranging bed clothes. She was not pretty, but to me she was an angel.

The disease left us as suddenly as it had come. One morning my mother and I both awoke feeling better than we had at any time we could easily remember. We knew, however, that this sort of euphoria was dangerous. Rumors about people who had had relapses from getting up too soon and had died suddenly were going around. So we obeyed Dr. Templeman's orders and stayed in bed a little longer.

On November 7 we heard some blowing of horns and whistles, and our first thought was that there was a fire. Our neighbors called out that an armistice had been signed in France. Then we heard that the rumor was false. But in the early morning hours of November 11 there was a greater din of whistles and gun shots. We then assumed that news of the end of the war had come and that it was real.

What a glorious day it was! It was a crisp, golden day and the war to end all wars was over, democracy had been saved, and there would be peace forever. The "boys" would soon be on the way back. Pack up your troubles in your old kit bag and smile, smile, smile. Roses might be blooming in Picardy away over there, but the Lord we'd be thanking, for the Yanks started yanking and yanked Kaiser Bill up a tree.—All the old cliches from the popular war songs were blending into a great hymn of joy at the end of a real-life symphony in which ugly noises had so long prevailed. And so everybody in Bayesville laughed and sang and walked about in delirious happiness on the streets and did absolutely no work. No cohesive kind of celebration, however, shaped up until late in the afternoon, when there seemed to be a simultaneous decision to make the arrival of the six o'clock train from Columbia the signal for a great jamboree at the station.

The arrival of the six o'clock train had, in fact, long been a kind of social event. Especially in the summer, people had become accustomed to strolling down to see the train come in and later to having ice cream at the Riddle Drug Store on the corner, or Fain's in the middle of the block, and then taking in the movie at the Ideal Theater across the street. The train had also been of some interest because it brought in the evening newspaper from Columbia. On this November 11, the evening paper would be of special significance because it would carry the full story of what had gone on in one of the most momentous happenings in modern history. In an era without radio or television, it is needless to say, the daily newspapers on special occasions were avidly awaited, and the cry of "Extra! Extra! Read all about it!" on the city streets always galvanized hearers into attention. So the arrival of the six o'clock train was a natural choice. I am sure that at the moment not many people knew that the agreement between the Germans and the Allies was signed in a railroad car in Compeigne forest, and thus that making our train a focal point of the celebration had a quaint appropriateness.

At any rate, so great was the occasion that I was bundled up sufficiently and allowed to go down to the station with the contingent on our block under the euphoric and irresponsible wing of Aunt Clarina, who had armed herself with a small dishpan and a long spoon from a preserving kettle for her noisemaker. Many other people arrived with pot and pans—enough to make a terrific din. And there were horns and bells of every shape, size, and sort—not to mention fire crackers, roman candles, and sparklers left over from the celebration of the previous Christmas. (It was not the local custom to celebrate the Fourth of July with fireworks; that is, other than rhetorical ones in political speeches.) The railroad track was completely blocked. Everybody yelled and screamed and blew or beat on whatever he had brought to make noise, and fireworks went off everywhere. People in the coaches got off and joined in the celebration. Some flasks were passed around, and a few beer bottles were in evidence, but most of the people were drunk with pure joy.

After a time the train conductor and the brakemen tried to clear the track and get the passengers back on the train. For some minutes their efforts looked like a lost cause. But then somebody produced a flag and began leading a parade down Railroad Avenue toward no discernible objective. Many people followed with their noise-makers. The crowd at the station began to thin, the track was open, and the passengers got back on the train.

There's no telling how late it was when it finally reached Augusta.

XI

VOYAGE TO GOTHAM

MY brother came home for the Christmas of 1918—the first time he had been there in almost two years. Among the things he brought me was a little book the size of a pocket reminder. It was bound in red leather for complimentary distribution by Rogers Peet and Company, and it was all about New York. I found it so absorbing that over the succeeding months I almost memorized it.

I could tell you, for example, details about the population and area of the city, the names of the boroughs, and the functions of most of the departments of city government. (Messrs. Rogers Peet and Company, however, did not encourage the inclusion in their book of things like Tammany Hall and wardheelers.) I could say glibly that New York had more Irishmen than Dublin (most of whom were in the police force), more Jews than Jerusalem, more Italians than Rome (or maybe it was Florence), though hardly more Englishmen than London which was the rival for the title of largest city in the world. I didn't figure that there could be more Germans than in Berlin, for I thought that all the Germans in the city might, like our Mr. Klask, have disappeared during the war to be perhaps transported back to their homeland via submarines. (I later found out that I was very wrong in this assumption, as I was in some others.) I knew all about the Statue of Liberty (designer, size, date of completion), Ellis Island, the Aquarium, the Bronx Zoo, the Metropolitan Opera House and Museum of Art, the Museum of Natural History, the Brooklyn Bridge, Grant's Tomb. I could recite some of the most important facts about that "Gothic cathedral of commerce" and "the tallest building in the world," the Woolworth Building, as well as about the red Byzantine tower that was runner-up in height, the Singer Building—one glorifying the dime and the other the sewing machine. I also knew about the Flat Iron Building and places like Times Square, Herald Square, Mott Street or China Town, and Mulberry Street, where the pushcart merchants were. The facts of the transportation systems I had also mastered to some extent: the number of miles of subway, B.M.T. and I.R.T.; the "El"; the Hudson Tubes; the surface trams; the double-decker Fifth Avenue buses; the ferries plying back and forth between New York and Jersey and Staten Island and other places. I could reel off information about the big stores: Macy's, Gimbal's, Hearn's, and John Wanamaker's—the last of which had many wonders in its great galleried central area. Moreover, there was a city under ground with shops, fruit stands, soda fountains, and restaurants, always open as if the sun never went up or down.

And the whole place was a splendid early model for the later Disney Land (which I, of course, could not have anticipated) existing just up the railroad track from where I lived. I knew this because a train coming from New York arrived in Bayesville every day at eleven o'clock in the morning and another from Augusta bound for New York arrived around three in the afternoon. It was called the "Augusta Special" and its long succession of Pullman cars with enchanting names like "Lake Placid" and "Pocahontas" added all but the ultimate glamor to our railroad accommodations. Indeed, from the initiation of the "special," train-watching became a more interesting sport than it had ever been before. The popularity of Augusta and the exclusiveness of Aiken as winter resorts filled the cars with all sorts of rich and fashionable people of whom we could at times get glimpses through the windows or on the observation platform. At other times we got a closer view when passengers for Aiken got off at Bayesville in preference to staying in their Pullmans, which had to be switched off to a branch line some twenty miles up the road and then pulled to their destination by a little engine like the Midlin. These interesting looking people with lots of luggage and polo and golf gear were met by chauffeurs in Packards, Rolls-Royces, Stutz Bearcats, Hispano-Suizas and more cars of other kinds than one could put down quickly in one's "car-collecting notebook." It was always thrilling to think that we might be seeing the Hitchcocks, the Iselins, the Graces, the Phippses, or the whole famous Meadowbrook Club team of Westbury, Long Island—Hitchcock, Milburn, Post, Knox, Von Stade, and the rest—that brought the world's best polo to the seven velvet-green fields in Aiken—no one of which was ever played on twice in the same week. Or even maybe somebody like the famous pianist Josef Hofmann would show up. Who could tell?

It was undoubtedly the Augusta Special (but for another reason) that put into my brother's head the notion of making my dream about the big city come true. "Why," he said one day at the dinner table, "why can't you let Buster come up to New York for a week or two next summer? It's all very easy. You just put him on the three o'clock train, and I will meet him the next morning in New York." At this point "Buster" was all ears. (He accepted this nickname only because big

"Brother" had given it to him.) "We'll see," said my father. "We'll see." My mother kept her usual skeptical silence. The matter seemed to be left at that. But not with "Buster" in whose none too spacious mind wheels would be set in motion not to cease until his objective had been reached.

It was a long time before summer, and I knew that I had work to do in two directions. I became my brother's best correspondent, writing him weekly letters either reciting to him what I had learned in the little red book or questioning him about things in New York that the book had not explained. On the home front I constantly reminded my father of how educational a trip to the big city would be for me and how really simple it was for me to get there. At school I announced to all my friends that I would spend part of the summer in New York City with the same air that I'd have assumed had I been announcing a coming voyage around the world or a summer in London, Paris, and Vienna. This particular ploy was a part of my plan to bring my dream to reality by the simple expedient of talking about it—a device that I had previously employed with some success. To one who had not traveled beyond forty miles or so in any direction from his home base, the whole project was actually something tremendous. Very few of my school mates had been so far, though various ones had been to Atlanta, Washington, and Charleston. "Buster," therefore, took care to make it plain that he'd be superior to them all when he came back to school in the fall.

Nothing got in the way of the tingling anticipation of the projected trip—not even a colorful event like the return of the Thirtieth ("Rainbow") Division, celebrated in Columbia with a big parade with thousands of soldiers, tanks, airplanes overhead (one of them fell, narrowly missing some of the crowd), bands, flags, bunting, and flowers. I went over with Aunt Clarina, who could not have been kept away since Jack with his corporal stripes and medals would be marching—fully or almost fully recovered from the gassing. I had always regarded Jack as a leprechaun more fitted to do an Irish jig (or a soft shoe or buck-and-wing bit that I had once seen him do in a local minstrel) than to fight. But there he was stepping along as precisely as the others and grinning archly. It was a great day for Aunt Clarina, and I enjoyed it because she did. But I kept telling myself that this was only an indifferent sort of prologue for the wonders to come in the summer.

The end of the school year came, however, without any crystallization of my plans. Much to my disgust nobody seemed to be thinking about them but me. Then one day Anna Maude announced out of a clear sky that the Wessons would be going to Washington in the last week of June. Elise had never really seen most of the important sights in the capital, and it was high time that she did. "If you are going to New York to see James," she said to me, "you could go on the train as far as Washington with us. Elise would like that. I'll talk to Uncle Paul." So she called my father, who in turn wrote my brother; and in a week the matter was settled. I would entrain (people entrained for important events; otherwise they merely boarded the train) at 3 o'clock on Friday, June 28, and my brother would meet me at the Pennsylvania Station in New York "without fail" (his words) at eleven o'clock on the morning of Saturday, June 29. Nothing could be plainer or simpler: Bayesville—New York, all in one package. My mother hesitated a little, doubting the wisdom of exposing one so untraveled and innocent as I to the perils of Babylon. But in the end she gave her consent.

Now to get ready! My standard summer dress-up outfit at home was a white blouse with four-in-hand tie, a pair of lightweight blue serge knickerbockers, sandals, and socks. Socks, my mother decided, could not be worn in the city. Black cotton stockings were proper. I also needed a Norfolk jacket, a raincoat, and a cap. Aunt Allie volunteered to take over the blouse or shirt department, making for me several white ones and a beautiful silk one with faint green and pink stripes on a white background. The Wessons found an almost new valise in their attic. I was completely outfitted and neatly packed by my mother three days before departure time.

But as the day approached my high enthusiasm underwent a transformation. I was overcome with fear and homesickness. New York now seemed far, far away, and it was a big city in which I could be easily swallowed up. In this thought I couldn't sleep at night and I agonized during the day. On June 27 I announced flatly to my father that I was not going. He laughed, but not at all unkindly; and putting his hand on my head, he said, "We can't back out now, can we? Think how disappointed James would be. Besides, you are thirteen years old—almost old enough to be a man." The die was cast. I was going, come what may.

My father, Aunt Clarina, and Jack walked to the train with me on the bright, warm Friday afternoon. My mother had waved goodbye to me from the front porch, electing not to make a public event of my going away. Aunt Allie closed the store for an hour and met us at the station. The Wessons were there when we arrived, having been driven down in their Buick by Joe Layton, and several of their friends were on hand to see them off. Just as the plumed black smoke of the engine appeared down the track, my father gave me my pocket book with eleven dollars in it and my return ticket in an envelope that I was to keep in my jacket pocket. He bade me be careful not to lose either. Aunt Clarina handed me the lunch that my mother had put up in a large, neatly wrapped package.

The great engine roared in with little clouds of steam about the wheels. I got hugs and kisses all around in some embarrassment. We looked for our Pullman car—K 40, the "Mount Pleasant." A porter took my bag and helped me in. Elise and I rushed to a vacant seat with a window on the station side so that we could wave out. And we were off.

I had a seat and an upper berth. The Wessons had a drawing room. I had never been inside a Pullman car before, and all the dark green plush and the whirring fans gave the whole scene a dramatic effect of affluence and luxury. Elise, who had been on Pullmans several times going to Atlanta and Charleston, undertook to show me around; and we finally made our way to the observation platform several cars back in order to watch the track reeling away behind us.

When we got back to the drawing room, Anna Maude pushed a button and gave an order to a porter who turned up promptly. Soon a waiter from the diner came in, put up a table, and served Coca-Colas. After that, a deck of cards appeared, and we played Set-Back. An hour or so passed quickly, and I began to think it time to break out the lunch boxes. But Anna Maude said that we would "tidy up" and go to the dining car for dinner. (At this time of the day it was always "supper" to me.)

Here again was drama. With scenery and telegraph poles rushing past and clicking wheels on the rails making a soothing music underneath us, eating was delightfully unreal. And all the silver and the finger bowls and all the other elaborate service!

We went to bed early in anticipation of getting up for an early morning breakfast before the Wessons got off at Washington. I watched the porter make down my berth with wonder, then climbed the little ladder, and managed after considerable effort and many contortions to strip to my B.V.D.'s. (My pajamas, alas, were in my bag under the bottom seat. No matter!) I allowed myself to be rocked, if not entirely gently, into a sleep of pure exhaustion and pleasure.

I regretted to say goodbye to the Wessons after I had breakfast with them and had them point out from the train window such sights of Washington as the Monument and the dome of the Capitol before the train went into the dark tunnel just before the station. But everything about the trip was so magic that I thought nothing of being alone for the rest of the way. Back in the car, I made friends with some of the other passengers, but I spent most of the time looking at a variety of places that skittered past and at the stations with such famous names as Baltimore, Wilmington, Philadelphia and Trenton.

As the train approached New York, my heart began beating faster and faster. At Manhattan Transfer I had my first glimpse of subway cars—above ground and grimy in the sunlight. Then we went into darkness, and I guessed that we were under the Hudson River. I had been over the Congaree on the railroad bridge to Columbia and over the Savannah on the railroad bridge just before Augusta. But never before under a river! The thought gave me pause. What if the water should come rushing down through a break somewhere?—But fear vanished in the contemplation of the miraculous situation in which I found myself.

A gentle black porter came, brushed me off with a whiskbroom, assisted me in putting on my jacket and cap, and got my valise for me. Grasping the valise firmly in one hand and the lunch package in the other, I sat perfectly still and erect, waiting properly to get off and meet my brother.

The train moved slowly and silently through the

darkness outside the windows and then came gently to a stop. I lined up in the aisle and then in the passageway with the other passengers and was finally assisted off the train—no steps to go down—by the porter, to whom I handed the silver half dollar that my father had told me to give him. When I looked up, I saw that I was on a dimly lit platform seething with people and seeming to stretch up and down for miles. I looked around for a welcoming hand and a smiling face. My brother had said "without fail." I remembered his very words from his letter, and I was saying them over and over to myself. But no brother was there. People were rushing back and forth, at times calling out to each other. Red Caps were hurriedly loading baggage and pushing it around in carts. I stood quietly for a moment. Then suddenly I was completely paralyzed, and cold sweat broke out on my forehead. The thing that I had feared had happened. I was lost.— People were jostling me in their haste. I had to do something; so with what seemed to be a tremendous effort I got myself into motion and followed the crowd, first along the platform, then up interminable steps, and up again to the enormous bright concourse of the station, looking as if the roof were as high as the sky and the expanse of the floor as great as a city. Still people, people, and no recognizable face anywhere. All strangers, strangers. What to do? What to do? Here at the end of a romantic journey was the horror of horrors—to be alone in a great wilderness of faceless human beings.

Finally, on a double-take I recognized three faces that had moved past without their seeing me or I them— a man, his wife, and little daughter who had been in my Pullman car. They were the Bennetts, and they were from Sylvania, Georgia. I knew because I had asked them. They were also on their first visit to New York. Here I felt was my only hope. So clutching my valise and lunch I ran after them, caught them, and explained my plight. By this time, I am afraid, there were tears in my eyes and I had all but lost my voice.

"Don't worry," Mr. Bennett said. "You'll go with us to our hotel, and we'll find your brother." With some relief but with no complete assurance, I climbed into a cab and took the short journey to the Martinique Hotel. (We could easily have walked!) All the magic of New York was gone. The place was a monster out to get me, just as a premonition had said it would!

I followed my benefactors into the hotel lobby and waited in a daze while they registered. Once up in their fifth-floor room, Mr. Bennett promptly said, "Now we'll see what we can do on the telephone." I gave him the number of my brother's place in Weehawken, which I had written down on a piece of paper in my jacket pocket. There was no answer to our ring. My apprehension grew. Then I produced the number of James's office in the manufacturing plant in Hoboken. This was a wan hope, for it was Saturday; and now that the war was over people were not working on Saturdays. The telephone at the other end of the line rang for what seemed to be an eternity. But Mr. Bennett hung on. Finally, somebody answered. It was a young assistant in the office who had just dropped in to get out some mail. No, he did not know how to reach my brother if he was not at home. But he would stand by in the office for an hour or more in the event that my brother called, and he would try to deliver some sort of message to the residence if no call came through. Mr. Bennett left the name of the hotel and the room number.

Nothing else could be done for the moment. So Mr. Bennett suggested that we all go out to lunch. I thanked him and declined, determined to stick by the phone at all odds as my only hope of ever being found again. After the Bennetts went out, misery descended like a blanket. I twitched and jerked and could not sit down. Though I was not hungry, I impulsively opened the lunch box. The sight of the fried chicken drumstick was too much to bear. My mother had fried it yesterday, but that was eons ago and she was millions of miles away in the misty distance. I remembered my father's saying that I was thirteen and almost a man. But homesickness is a relentless, ravaging foe of rationality, and it was useless to argue myself out of the abyss into which it had plunged me. As I look back on it, I think that the most pathetic picture of myself that I could possibly paint would be that of my gnawing a chicken drumstick while, with tears rolling down my cheeks, I gazed out of a sooty hotel window on angular, hostile buildings around me and on antlike people as they scurried along on the street below—all in a sickening yellowish light. Not one of Doré's illustrations for Dante's Hell excelled it in the depiction of the hopeless lost.

Then the telephone rang. The sound was jarring, but it was golden. "Buster," came the voice on the line, "is that you?" Had I been older than I was, I'd have said, "You're damn well right it is. And where in the hell are you?" But at the time I had never considered using such sinful language; thus I merely exclaimed "Brother!" "What about meeting me at the corner of Thirty-Third Street and Broadway?" the jokester came back. "No thank you," I said. "I am not leaving this room." I put down the receiver and rushed into the bathroom, washed my face, and combed my hair with a pocket comb. I was not going to let my brother see that I had been crying. In a few minutes I calmly let him in at the door.

He had a lot of explaining to do, but he was not apologetic. The train had come in from Washington in three sections. I was not on the first or the second. While he was sitting for the third, he "met an old friend" who had persuaded him to dash into the Savarin Bar for a "quick one." When he realized that the third section had come in some minutes before it was scheduled and that he had just missed it, he looked for me at the big information desk in the center of the concourse. (How could I have known to go there? Nobody had told me.) He then called his office and got the information Mr. Bennett had phoned in. He walked over to the Martinique and called me on the house phone. It was just as simple as that. To him—not to me. I was still terribly shaken, but I was determined.not to let him see that I was. So I said a prayer of thanks to heaven for the luck that rescued me, and I made up my mind to be happy again.

We didn't wait for the Bennetts to come back. James wrote a nice note on hotel stationery to thank them and left it by the telephone. I never saw them again. But I never forgot them. I hope they had a good time in New York.

The memory of my agony was all but gone as we made our way across town to the slip of the Weehawken Ferry, moved thrillingly across the busy river in bright sunshine (my first boat trip ever), and arrived at my brother's house. It was not only situated on the Palisades near the spot where Alexander Hamilton and Aaron Burr had fought but it also commanded a perfect view of the whole panorama of Manhattan. What a sight! The magic of the metropolis was restored. I decided that it exceeded my fondest dreams. And it was to be all mine for two weeks!

Events seemed designed to make my visit memorable on a scale far larger than a purely private one. For example, the weekend of my arrival was the last before the Wartime Prohibition Act was scheduled to go into effect. At noon on Monday my brother took me to a saloon just around the corner from his office where a free-lunch counter was still in operation. This was a gesture designed as part of his idea of allowing me to feel almost like a grown-up and also of letting me experience an institution that seemed slated for oblivion—though I assumed from the way it was functioning that nobody believed that it wouldn't be there forever. I had a roast-beef sandwich on rye, washed down with an orange soda. I had tasted beer at home once when a doctor had prescribed lager to my mother for a run-down condition, and I had not liked it. I am not sure that the bartender would have wanted to serve me beer anyway.

I knew relatively little about Prohibition, but I was not a "Pussyfoot" Johnson and I really thought that I didn't approve of it. I had long revoked the pledge and the white ribbon into which I had been led under the influence of Miss Millie Barton (*requiescat cum signo fidei et in somno pacis*). My comic cousin, Jack Connor, who had known the joys of wine, women, and song as a "doughboy" in "gay Paree," had expressed himself indignantly about a Congress that had so "betrayed" the "boys" who were fighting and dying overseas as to let Andrew Volstead get his legislation enacted. The Wartime Prohibition Act (not the Eighteenth Amendment which was to come later and be worse) may have been designed to keep the soldiers at home from evil ways, but the effect was to take the cheer out of the homecoming ones who had been standing all the gaff in France. So Jack argued as he taught me a little drinking song that ran—

> Bon jour, ma chérie,
> Comment allez-vous?
> Bon jour, ma chérie,
> Just tell me how are you?
> Avez-vous fiancé, gentil Américain?
> Voulez-vous coucher avec moi ce soir?
> Oui, oui!
> Trés bien.

If my mother had understood bad French, she would have tanned both Jack and me for this sinful combination of drink and sex. But as for me, at my present age I thought it much better than "Sur le pont d'Avignon," that I used to sing in school, and I agreed with Jack's main argument about Prohibition, too.

On the night of June 30 my brother took me over to Manhattan, where we did a lot of walking just to see the lights and the people. In some areas there was a great bustle, producing a scene that I had not anticipated. Long drays loaded with great hogsheads were being drawn in considerable numbers by huge Percheron or Clydesdale horses. And when the drays were unloaded, the hogsheads were rolled along the streets to disappear in basement doors. An air of urgency and seriousness was pervasive. And in places where the lights were not too bright and mist was in the air, the scene looked like something from a D.W. Griffith movie.

So far as the other "sights" of the city were concerned, I had provided my brother with a list just to be sure that I should not miss anything important. He could not take off enough time from business to do everything for me; so he cannily enlisted some assistants. The ablest was a middle-aged cousin named Dan McQueen, a minister who had married a rich wife in East Orange and had retired from the battlefields of the Lord to live the good life. He was Christian martyr enough, nevertheless, to see me through the Aquarium, far downtown, to transport me via a Fifth Avenue bus (a "must" on my list of modes of transportation to be sampled) and subway to the Bronx Zoo, away uptown, and to conduct me through it. Two lovely secretaries of German extraction, brunette Katherine Grimm and blonde Lillian Meissner, took time off to give me short tours.

James arranged a trip to Coney Island by boat one

night; and on another night he threw in Palisades Park for good measure. He took a girl friend along (at thirty he was as yet unmarried); but I wasn't interested, and I was inclined to feel that a second go at an amusement park was a work of supererogation. I had more serious things to do and see. It wasn't the season for the Metropolitan Opera. But since I had never seen a stage show, I mentioned the "Ziegfeld Follies" at the New Amsterdam and the "George White Scandals" at the Liberty as things that would indubitably contribute to my education. My brother thought otherwise; and we settled, if I remember correctly, for a Broadway movie, the recently opened sad *Broken Blossoms.*

A Fourth of July excursion included an overnight visit to the McQueens in their enormous red brick Victorian house on Prospect Avenue in East Orange. The house was larger than Aunt Elise's by far and the servants, unlike my favorites Mary Wayne and Joe Layton, were white. They appeared to be zombies to me and their formality was so stifling that it made me uneasy. Cousin Edith was as gracious and kind as she could be. But she looked much older than Dan; and she was very pallid and pasty surrounded as she seemed to be with lace and filmy scarves, just as she might have appeared in the drawings of Mary Petty or Helen Hokinson. All the time I kept feeling that formal entertainment was not an objective of my trip north; and I wanted to return as quickly as possible to the living world outside a dead house.

We were off the next day for Asbury Park and my first view of the ocean. In Bayesville it had been less than two hundred miles away all the time, but nobody had taken me to see it. And here it was up in New Jersey—the Atlantic, all full of waves and whitecaps and sea shells, just as it had been billed. The boardwalk, the wicker chairs pushed along it, the amusement piers, and the salt-water taffy were all just as I had read they would be. And here they were, and here I was. It was all too remarkable. But the most wonderful event, the climax of all, was still to come—and soon.

While I was bathing in the Atlantic, in fact, President Wilson was on the same ocean returning from the Peace Conference in Paris. As I knew from the newspapers, he had sailed on the U.S. Transport *George Washington* on Monday, June 30—the very day on which I was watching the considerable to-do being made to circumvent the Wartime Prohibition Act. I had long been an ardent admirer of the President. All during the war, my admiration for him had grown. I had seen his picture on numerous posters, in *Leslie's Magazine,* and the *Literary Digest,* and even in the movies in the Pathé News. At first he had "kept us out of the war"; and once we were in he had "led us to victory"—or, in his most recent words, to what he most desired: namely, "peace without victory." I saw no contradiction and I found no fault. I knew something about his plan for a "League of Nations" and about his "Fourteen Points"—though not very much; and I had read about his first triumphal tour abroad as the "savior of Europe." I could name the "Big Four" of the Peace Conference: Lloyd-George, Clemenceau, Orlando, Wilson. I felt that Wilson towered over the lot of them like a Gulliver over the Lilliputians. In fact, I was ready to believe that he was not only the greatest living man but the greatest man of all time, falling just respectfully and unsacrilegiously short of the Persons of the Trinity.

In the *Digest* there had been a cartoon showing him as a dapper suitor with a big, fat girl-friend labeled "U.S. Senate," the latter grimacing because the former had not sent her even a postcard from Paris; and there was yet another cartoon in which a rolled document labeled "U.S. Constitution" was unsuccessfully trying to sit on the same chair with a document labeled "The League Covenant." "No Room for Both" ran the caption. But these signs of coming trouble for my hero went over my head. Hero he was, and hero he would remain.

I was all set for the triumphal entry on Tuesday, July 8, and I was willing to believe that my whole expedition to the North was made with this occasion as its objective.

On the Monday before the arrival of the George Washington, I had cased the drab area of the Hoboken docks. It was not very far from my brother's office; and Gus Meissner, the handsome sixteen-year-old brother of one of my favorite secretaries had offered to be my guide. Though we could not get on the piers, here and there I had a good look at ships still in their warpaint or camouflage, including the huge hulk of the Leviathan, certainly the largest floating thing that I ever imagined I might see. Gus explained that it had been the Vaterland of the North German Lloyd Line before it had been confiscated by us during the war and had been appropriately renamed. This knowledge added to the patriotic ferver that I was rapidly developing over our victory and the approach of the man who had engineered it.

If I had had my way, on Tuesday, July 8—my version of Der Tag—I'd have been on board one of the four dreadnoughts and thirty-six destroyers that sailed out to meet the presidential ship off Sandy Hook—or at least on one of the planes flying escort overhead. But since I had not yet made the acquaintance of the Honorable Josephus Daniels, Secretary of the Navy, I had no way of arranging such. I could not get anybody interested even in getting me aboard one of the sight-seeing boats or tugs that I knew would be in the harbor and in the river.

I at least wanted to get down to the parade route on River Street as early as possible in the morning. My brother, on the other hand, ruled that we would take our stations there early in the afternoon; and to get me out of his way he sent me with one of the office boys to the roof of the factory where I could have a good view of the Hudson and the traffic on it.

When we got to River Street shortly after noon, we had to push and squeeze our way through the crowds that had been there, as I anticipated, practically since dawn. Banners, flags, and bunting lined the street as far as I could see, happily masking its ugliness. Hawkers were everywhere selling flags, badges, banners, noise-makers, confetti, soft drinks, nuts, candy. The din was terrific. I got a little silk flag which had a red border and a blue star on a white center, overprinted with "Welcome Home!" in black letters. (No palm branches were available!)

Around two o'clock there was the sound of guns firing in the distance. The harbor forts were saluting, and the air in River Street became electric. My brother and I had pushed and squeezed up until we had a fairly good view of the parade route, but I wished I were back on the factory roof so that I could see the grand procession of fighting ships led by the flagship *Pennsylvania* as it escorted the *George Washington* up the Hudson. I simply had to imagine what was going on.

Planes became more numerous over the city and the docks. And suddenly there came the sharp report of aerial bombs. The presidential ship, somebody informed me, was now even with the pierhead where it was to dock. It was about three o'clock. In half an hour the President had stepped upon American "soil" again—though I knew that it must have been wood or concrete that his foot touched. I could not see or hear the shipyard band in overalls that greeted him or the crisply uniformed Q.M.C. girls lined up in formation in front of him, all symbolic of our united effort in winning the war. The *Times,* however, had said that they would be there, and I was sure that they were. The ten thousand school children were there as advertised, I was also sure—every one of them, all in white and massed to contribute their special bit to the occasion. I could hardly see anything else but them. Hysterical cheering and shouting up the street announced that the cavalcade with an open red car carrying the President was finally approaching. He was coming! The crowds grew wilder and wilder and the noise louder. The school children got ready to follow a director on an elevated stand in a mighty patriotic chorus of some sort. But as the red car came into view, somebody rushed out and presented a bouquet. Pandemonium took over. Everybody shouted wildly and waved flags or handkerchiefs. Nobody raised a tune.

I yelled, waved, and screamed, too, completely caught up in the overpowering emotion of the occasion. Then I stood transfixed. Here within a few feet of me appeared the great President of the United States, as big as life with his silk top hat, his long nose on a chiseled face, and pince-nez glasses, just as I had seen him in a hundred photographs. Mrs. Wilson was there, too, looking queenly in a curious hat like a mixing bowl upside down; and there was an admiral in a gleaming uniform of summer dress whites. But the other two mattered not at all. I saw them only from the corner of my eye. My real focus was on the Great Man alone.

What a stupendous occasion! Back in Bayesville I never dreamed that I'd experience anything like it.

The big red car moved on, and with its movement a wave of cheers seemed to roll down the street. Past where I was standing other cars came, filled with men in black suits and silk hats, and Army and Navy officers with fancy hats and caps with gold on them, epaulets, and gold braid. People cheered them, too, and waved flags at them. The airplanes were still flying about overhead.

Over the din came some deep-throated whistles from the harbor. More and more cars came till there was the last one with a band following. Then everybody seemed to rush into the street to follow the parade.

I stood quite still for a time, not willing to change any part of my experience. For a moment I thought of Damon and wished that he could have seen what I saw. But I forgot him at the touch of my brother's hand: the signal that we, too, should go.

I suppose deep down I knew that I was just a young hayseed from the provinces—a little pretentious and vain, not overly bright, immature even for my few years. But I could not help intuiting that something had gone on that would be a watershed in my personal history. I had been told by somebody that in the Catholic Church seven was the age of reason and that at twelve a person could take up the banner of Faith in confirmation. At fourteen, I had also heard, English and American law could hold me responsible for my actions. My father said that I was approaching manhood. Maybe that is what I was doing.

"Heaven lies about us in our infancy," Wordsworth said. History does, I'd have said. Or so I later figured. For me at the age of thirteen history had always been "out there" to be heard about or to be read about in my fumbling way or to be reenacted in games—but not really to be experienced. After all, I might have concluded, history like news was all bad. Witness the big events, many of them holocausts and tragedies, that had seemed to bracket my key birthdays: the San Francisco earthquake and fire preceding my first; the sinking of the *Titanic* my sixth; the Great War in Europe with its terrible slaughter beginning hard upon my eighth birthday—all fortunately remote. Now for the first time I had caught up with history in a real, honest-to-goodness view of the man who during a large part of my lifetime had seemed to make most of it. And the vision that I got was good, not bad—for it promised peace and happiness not only for me but for the whole world. Indeed, here was history in front of me. I was still seeing it with my own eyes. And, more important, I sensed that in the simple act of shouting and waving my flag in the direction of the world's greatest man, I had participated in it.

Years later I discovered that Alexander Pope had written:

> Heaven from all creatures hides the book of Fate,
> All but the page prescrib'd, their present state.

True perhaps, but no matter! There on River Street in Hoboken on July 8, 1919, I needed only the prescribed page. So much so that even from the vantage point of half a century it seems cruel to remind myself of the prophetic words of those daft and canny British authors of a great anti-history called *1066 and All That* to the effect that in the "Chamber of Horrors" at Versailles Mr. Wilson had actually achieved the peace to end all peace.

At any rate on July 12 when I stepped out of my dream and onto the station platform once again in Bayesville, I felt that I was quite a different person from the one who had left it such a long and such a short time ago. I carried my valise with firm assurance, and I confidently held a well-wrapped package from Macy's containing presents for as many members of my family as I could afford to bring them to. My father did not come to the station, for it was Saturday and his busy time at the store. He had asked my cousin Jack to do the honors. The Wessons who had returned home a few days before did considerably more. They sent Joe Layton in his chauffeur's cap and broad grin in the shiny dark green Buick sedan that looked for all the world like a show case.

So Jack and I rode in some grandeur to the modest

BIOGRAPHICAL NOTE

LODWICK HARTLEY, a native South Carolinian, has been a longtime resident of North Carolina. He holds degrees from Furman, Columbia, and Princeton universities and was formerly head of the English Department at North Carolina State University.

His six books and numerous articles are chiefly devoted to literary biography and criticism. His poetry and short stories have appeared in some of the leading Southern literary magazines. One of his stories has appeared in the O. *Henry Memorial Prize Stories.*

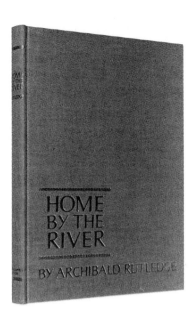

HOME BY THE RIVER

by Archibald Rutledge

The story of Hampton Plantation, set against the background of Southern coastland along the broad Santee River, from colonial beginnings to its loving restoration by the author, South Carolina's poet laureate. As only a poet can, Rutledge describes a man's love for his heritage, sharing his rediscovery of the mystical beauty and historic charm of his ancestral home—still a sanctuary for man and wildlife—and his pleasure in its people. "A delightful chronicle."—*New York World Telegram* "... superb chapters on the birds, the rodents, the reptiles, the amphibians, game and wildfowl with which his 2,000 acres abound."—*Boston Traveler.*

Cloth, 200 pages, 7 x 10, $10.00
26 b/w illustrations
ISBN 0-87844-028-3